# Praise for *Max Einstein: The Genius Experiment*

'James Patterson is the Einstein of fiction and has solved the equation for storytelling: Adventure + Science = AWESOME!' TOM FLETCHER

'Any young readers out there interested in science and adventure... this book is brilliant!' TIM PEAKE

'An inspirational page-turner that won't let you down. This book celebrates the importance of young people's new ideas and endless imaginations' RACHEL IGNOTOFSKY, AUTHOR OF *WOMEN IN SCIENCE*

'A fast-paced, science-filled caper' *WALL STREET JOURNAL*

'This story is packed with excitement and has a brilliant heroine in Max' *THE WEEK JUNIOR*

'Max Einstein is everything you hope young girls can dream to be: smart, brave, creative, and able to inspire others to be the same. I love this book for all kids who want to dream big!' MAYIM BIALIK, AUTHOR OF *GIRLING UP* AND *BOYING UP*

'Give this book to the future scientist in your life!' JENNIFER L. HOLM, AUTHOR OF *THE FOURTEENTH GOLDFISH*

'If you're interested in science, mysteries, or courageous heroines, this is a must-read!' CHELSEA CLINTON

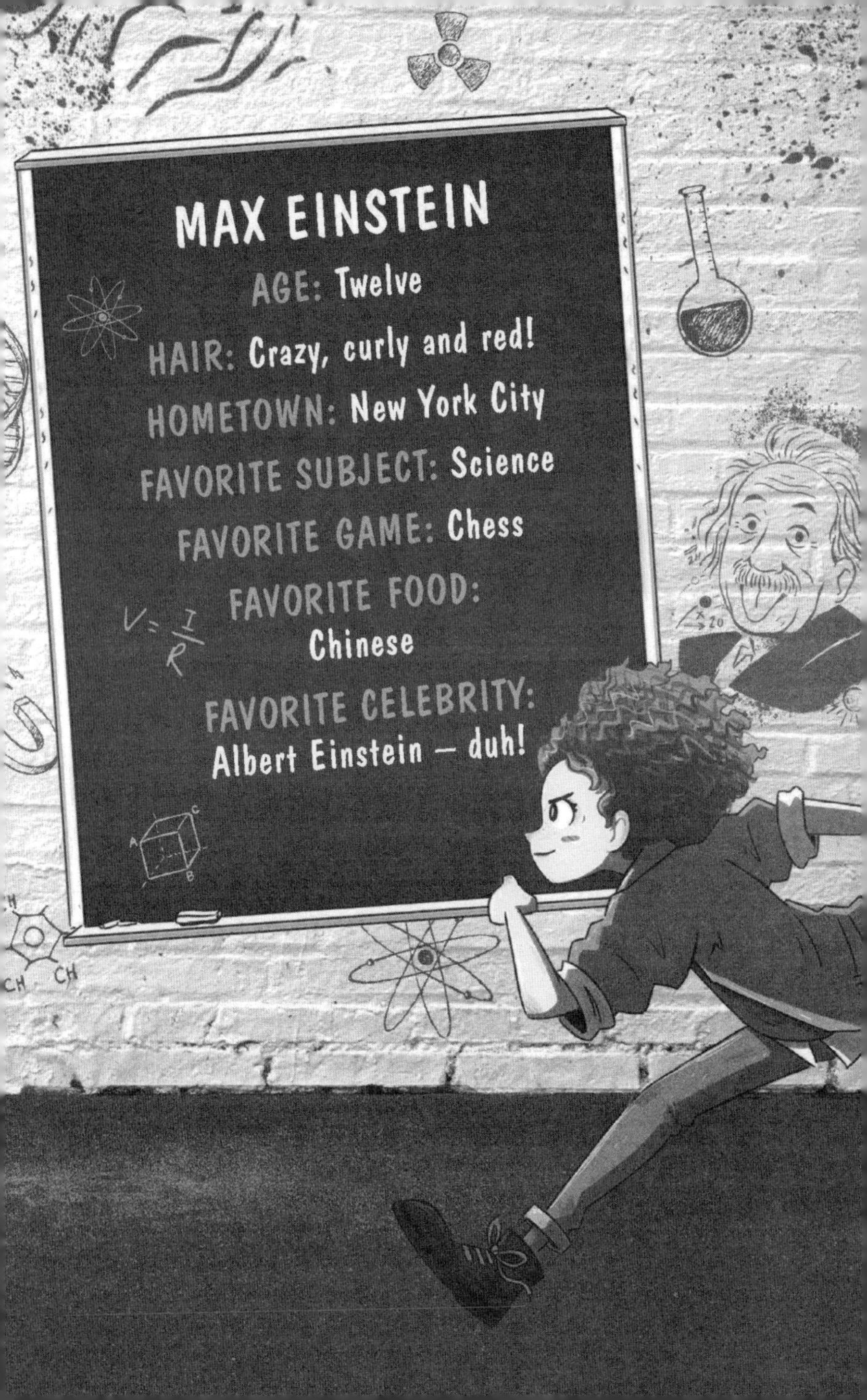

MAX EINSTEIN
AGE: Twelve
HAIR: Crazy, curly and red!
HOMETOWN: New York City
FAVORITE SUBJECT: Science
FAVORITE GAME: Chess
FAVORITE FOOD:
Chinese
FAVORITE CELEBRITY:
Albert Einstein – duh!

# MAX
# EINSTEIN
## SAVES THE FUTURE

# JAMES PATTERSON
### and Chris Grabenstein

## Illustrated by Beverly Johnson

1 3 5 7 9 10 8 6 4 2

Young Arrow
20 Vauxhall Bridge Road
London SW1V 2SA

Young Arrow is part of the Penguin Random House group of companies whose
addresses can be found at global.penguinrandomhouse.com

Copyright © Zero Point Ventures LLC. 2020
Illustrations copyright © Hachette Book Group, Inc. 2020

James Patterson has asserted his right to be identified as the author of this Work in
accordance with the Copyright, Designs and Patents Act 1988

First published in Great Britain by Young Arrow in 2020

www.penguin.co.uk

A CIP catalogue record for this book is available from the British Library

ISBN 9781529119640
ISBN 9781529119657 (trade paperback edition)

Printed and bound in Great Britain by Clays Ltd, Elcograf S.p.A.

Penguin Random House is committed to a sustainable future for
our business, our readers and our planet. This book is made from
Forest Stewardship Council® certified paper

MIX
Paper from
responsible sources
FSC® C018179

# MAX
# EINSTEIN
## SAVES THE FUTURE

# The Story So Far...

**Max Einstein is not your typical twelve-year-old** genius.

She hacked the computer system at NYU so she could attend college classes. She built inventions to help the homeless people she lived with.

She talks with her hero, Albert Einstein. (Okay, that's just in her imagination.)

But everything changed when Max, a homeless orphan who'd never known her parents, was recruited by a mysterious organization known as the Change Makers Institute! Their mission: solve some of the world's toughest problems using science. She led a diverse group of young geniuses from around the globe as they invented new ways to bring electricity to the farthest reaches of the planet and cleaned up an Indian village's water supply.

But they can only continue to do good in the world if the sinister outfit known as the Corp doesn't get to Max and her new friends first.

Because they'll do whatever it takes to stop Max and her team of do-gooders.

$$t' = \frac{t}{\sqrt{1 - \frac{v^2}{c^2}}}$$

$t'$ = change in time
$t$ = rest time
$v$ = velocity
$c$ = speed of light

" I never think about the future..
It comes soon enough."
-Albert Einstein

# Prologue

*1921*
*Princeton, New Jersey, USA*

**The young couple placed their baby daughter in a** cardboard box lined with a soft, brown flannel blanket.

"Stay put," cooed the mother.

"We're expecting a very special guest this evening," added the father.

The mother nodded. "Our mentor! The one who got all of this started!"

She swept open her arms to take in the strange collection of electronic contraptions and lab equipment set up in the basement of their modest home on Battle Road, not far from the Princeton University campus, where both husband and wife were distinguished professors.

As physicists, they were extremely creative and inventive. Which is why the two geniuses created a playpen for their daughter out of a cardboard box.

The baby loved it. She smiled and gurgled and settled into her fuzzy blanket, watching her parents bustle around the room. They spun dials, tapped buttons, and shoved levers into their upright "on" positions—setting off a colorful array of blinking lights.

The baby *ooh*ed and brought her pudgy hands together. She stared at the blinking lights.

Soon, the whole basement began to hum.

"I suspect Professor Einstein will be impressed," offered the father.

"I hope so," said the mother. "After all, he inspired our experiment. This is all because of him."

Back when the brilliant father and mother were graduate students at Princeton University (two of the youngest ever because they were both considered child prodigies), they'd heard the distinguished Albert Einstein give a lecture about general relativity. They'd been working on its practical applications ever since.

The thrum of turbo-charging electricity and spinning magnetos in the basement was now so loud, the couple almost didn't hear the doorbell ringing upstairs.

"It's him!" exclaimed the father. "He's here. Professor Einstein himself!"

"Did you remember to pick up the orange cake and strawberries?" asked the mother as they both hurried to the basement's wooden staircase.

"Yes, dear. We'll need to whip the cream ..."

"We can do that after our demonstration!"

They hurried up the steps to greet their guest, leaving their baby alone in the basement, mesmerized by all the strange sounds and the bright rainbow of blinking lights.

She crawled out of the cardboard box and made her way across the cold concrete floor, which seemed to be growing even colder as frost appeared on the *insides* of the basement's windows.

The baby scuttled around stacks of wooden crates and made a beeline toward an open suitcase.

Taped to its open lid was a glossy photograph of a man with funny, frizzy hair. The shiny portrait reflected the dazzling light show and drew the baby closer. There was some kind of scholarly paper tucked into the suitcase as well. The baby, of course, couldn't read what was written on it. All she wanted was to reach out and touch all the brilliant lights twinkling and dancing on the friendly face of the white-haired old man.

The water pipes in the basement ceiling groaned and rattled as they froze.

The windows were now caked with two inches of ice.

The baby could see her own foggy breath.

Suddenly, there was a flash of blindingly bright light. An arc of indoor lightning.

The noise ceased.

The cold vanished.

And the baby girl's whole world would never be the same.

# The Present
# London, England

# 1

Max Einstein strode through the fog of London, her open trench coat flapping behind her like a superhero's cape.

Her mop of curly red hair was even frizzier than usual because, as she of course knew, the chemistry of human hair made it susceptible to changes in the amount of hydrogen present in the air and that, of course, was directly linked to humidity because all that foggy, airborne water was made up of two hydrogen atoms per molecule.

Thinking about the chemistry of her hair kept her mind occupied. For about two seconds.

Then Max was bored again.

She was in London impatiently awaiting the next Change Makers Institute assignment from the program's benefactor, Benjamin Franklin Abercrombie, whom Max just called Ben. Hey, even though he was a bajillionaire, he was only two years older than Max. He was also extremely cute. And she especially approved of the way he spent his money—funding a league of kid geniuses to tackle the world's problems without any interference from governments. How awesome was that?

Max thought about Ben for maybe a nanosecond then flipped back to being bored and frustrated because Newton's first law of motion, sometimes called the law of inertia, never seemed to apply to twelve-year-old Max Einstein. Newton stipulated that an object at rest stays at rest while an object in motion stays in motion.

The problem? Max Einstein didn't know how to rest. She craved action. Constant forward motion. Staying inert just wasn't her thing.

Her mind flitted back to her decision not to wear a knit hat as she traipsed around London—some kind of disguise to keep her frizzy, floppy tangle of red curls out of sight because her hair was something of a homing beacon for any nefarious villains who might be searching for her.

And they were.

A shadowy group that called themselves the Corp was very interested in recruiting Max and her extremely high IQ to switch sides and play for their team. Even if it meant kidnapping her. Fortunately, Max's London roommate, who used to work for the evildoers before he had a major change of heart, advised her that, according to his vast network of undisclosable contacts, "The Corp has no idea that either of us is currently situated in London, England."

Leo, her roommate, always called it "London, England," even though nobody else did. He was just a little odd that way.

With Leo's assurance that she'd be safe, Max had decided to make her waiting time in London not feel like a waste of time. She would boldly venture outside of her cramped flat (what Londoners called an apartment) in a youth hostel (Ben's choice) and visit all the spots in the city that her hero, Albert Einstein, had also visited when he was in London. She would occupy the same space, though not the same time, that the great genius had occupied. Maybe, Max figured, it would somehow bring them closer. Even if it didn't, the experiences would be fun and educational. And like Dr. Einstein said, "The only source of knowledge is experience."

Max longed to experience at least one new thing every day.

That's why she was marching through the fog, headed for someplace she'd never been before: the Royal Albert Hall. Located in London's South Kensington district, it was opened by Queen Victoria in 1871 and named in memory of her husband, Prince Albert. It was home to nearly four hundred performances each year, everything from rock and pop concerts to classical music and ballet to award ceremonies. Celebrated names from the hall's history who were honored with stars and engravings around the outside of the building included Adele, Eric Clapton, Winston Churchill, Muhammad Ali, and, of course, close to door 5, Albert Einstein.

There was a concert that night, though Max didn't have a ticket.

But she didn't think she'd need one to get in.

Because she was in possession of something that she was confident would become her secret all-access pass.

# 2

Einstein once said that "reality is merely an illusion, albeit a very persistent one."

So Max had decided to create her own illusion of reality. That's why she was carrying an empty violin case, which was also a small tribute to her hero. Albert Einstein started taking violin lessons when he was six years old and continued playing his whole life. He named his violin "Lina" and could play Mozart sonatas beautifully. Music, he said, helped him when he was thinking about his theories or working on a thought experiment.

Now Max hoped music would help her sneak into the Royal Albert Hall.

"Excuse me," she said to the first security guard she saw. "Where's the musicians' entrance?"

Mozart and Bach made music with clarity, simplicity, and matrematical precision — the same things Einstein put into his theories.

I live my daydreams in music!

She wiggled the violin case to make certain the guard noticed she was carrying one.

"Stage Door. Just around the bend there, past door number one. You can't miss it. Cheers."

"Thanks!" Max didn't feel guilty about tricking the guard. She never *said* she was a musician. She just let him create that particular illusion of reality all by himself, and she didn't even have to be very persistent about it.

The stage door allowed Max to skip the crowds lining up at the main entrance and, of course, the ticket takers. She acted like she knew what she was doing and, in no time, was standing backstage in the darkness of the wings.

*This is where Einstein stood,* she told herself.

*No, I was a little bit to the left,* replied Einstein.

Einstein wasn't *really* there. This was just something Max did from time to time. She had wonderful, unspoken conversations with the imaginary Einstein in her head. To her, he wasn't just a world-renowned genius—he was a funny, grandfatherly figure with a wicked sense of humor.

But standing right where (or close to where) her idol had stood on October 3, 1933, gave her goose bumps. That night, Professor Einstein spoke to a packed house about his fears for the looming crisis in Europe, where Adolf Hitler and fascism were on the rise. It was six years before World

War II, but to Einstein and other Jews living in Germany the horror was already very real.

Being in the same space where Einstein had been at a different time made Max muse about looking for a wrinkle in the boundaries of space and time. Wouldn't it be great to step across that wrinkle and go back in time to meet her hero? He'd been here then. She was here now. If only their timelines could somehow overlap and intersect!

Then, maybe, together they could find another wrinkle in time and leap into the future, so Max could see what it held for her. Or maybe, Dr. Einstein could show her how to travel twelve years *backward* in time so she could finally figure out who her parents were.

Max had been an orphan for what seemed like her entire life. She had some vague memories of her parents. But they were fuzzy. The gray and blurry kind you can almost but not quite recall from your crib.

Even if Dr. Einstein couldn't do all that, Max could at least warn him about the Nazi bounty hunters shadowing him on his 1933 London visit.

*I read about it,* she said to her imaginary Einstein. *There was a plot to assassinate you while you were here.*

*Ah,* replied the Einstein in her head, *but it wasn't a very good plot, was it? I survived until 1955! And don't you think it's nice that they call this the Royal Albert Hall? It was so kind of them to name it after me.*

Max smiled. She loved it when the Einstein in her head made one of his corny jokes. It made him feel even more like a grandfather, something she'd never had.

*Are bad people still following you, Maxine?* Einstein asked.

*Yes. The goons from the Corp. But, don't worry—they're not here in London.*

And, of course, the instant she said that, two burly men dressed all in black stepped out of the shadows toward her.

# 3

"What are you doing back here, young lady?" asked one of the men. He had a curly communicator wire coming out of his ear. He also had arm muscles the size of most people's thighs. His pumped-up partner looked exactly like him, except with a blond buzz cut instead of a brown one.

Max thought about replying, *I'm communing with my muse,* but she didn't think the two men, who were wearing black SECURITY T-shirts, would appreciate that answer. So she held up her violin case again.

"I'm a musician?" Yes, she said it like a question, which is seldom a convincing way to give an answer.

"Is that so?" said the blond buzz cut. "Violin?"

Max nodded.

"Don't remember a capella groups such as this evening's

performers using violins. Typically, they just use their mouths."

Max glanced to her left. A group of six singers had stepped into the wings. None of them were carrying a musical instrument.

"Let's go, miss," said the brown-haired bouncer, gently taking Max by the arm and escorting her toward the exit. "I'd love to let you see the show for free, but then I'd most likely lose my job. Cheers."

Two minutes later, Max was back on the street outside the Royal Albert Hall. It was probably a street that Albert Einstein had walked but it just didn't have the same magical feeling as being backstage.

Frustrated, Max stepped into one of London's red phone booths (which didn't have a phone in it) and pulled an encrypted satellite phone out of her trench coat's deep side pocket.

It was time to call Ben. Fortunately, Max had his direct number. (He'd also paid for the very expensive Iridium Extreme satellite phone.)

Ben answered on the third ring. He always answered on the third ring.

"Um, hello, Max," he said, without asking who was calling. Max figured he had the most sophisticated caller ID system in the universe. "How's, you know, London?"

"Boring."

"Seriously? London? The one in England? There's so much to do and see…"

"When do we start our next project?"

"Soon, Max. Be patient. I'm doing some very extensive research. This will be your biggest challenge yet. We don't want you to jump into it unprepared."

"Soon?"

"Right. Just, you know, hang tight. I'll get back to you. Soon."

Max terminated the call.

*Soon.*

It was one of those words that proved the relativity of time.

For many children, "soon" seemed like forever when it was Christmas Eve and they couldn't open their presents until Christmas morning. For others, it seemed like an instant when the dentist came into the waiting room and said she'd see you "soon."

Max was definitely in the Christmas Eve category. Soon seemed like forever.

Resigned to waiting, she began strolling back to the youth hostel near Hyde Park where she and Leo had their flat, which was, basically, a college dormitory room.

She saw a man pushing a grocery cart filled to the brim

with plastic-wrapped sandwiches. Curious, she followed him as he rattled his cart down a cobblestone alleyway that was lit by a single misty streetlamp.

"Evening, Franky," the man said to a shadowy lump on the ground. "How's the family?"

The rumpled lump stirred. Max realized it was a man in a sleeping bag. As her eyes adjusted to the darkness, she could see a clump of sleeping bags. Some quite small.

"Suppertime!" said the man cheerfully, dipping into his cart and pulling out a stack of shrink-wrapped sandwiches. "Sorry to be so late. Had to wait for the shop to close for the day. Wiltshire cured ham on malted bread for you and the missus. Bacon sandwiches for the kids."

"Thank you, Charles," said the man who'd been sleeping with his family in the alleyway.

Two little heads popped up from the bedding at the mention of food, and Max could make out their big smiles, despite their humble sleeping space. Kids were resilient, she knew, but seeing their little hands reach eagerly for the sandwiches broke her heart a little.

She was that kid, once.

When Max was living on the streets of New York City, finding food had been her primary objective every day. The quest sometimes led Max to eat things not as clean and neatly packaged as the sandwiches Charles was passing out.

She guessed they were the ones his shop couldn't sell before closing.

Max carefully backed out of the alley. She didn't want the homeless family seeing her. Especially the kids.

She remembered the embarrassment and humiliation she sometimes used to feel while scrounging for food. Those emotions were strong. But not as strong as the hunger pangs in her belly.

# 4

When Max finally arrived home at her apartment building, she said hello to some of the other students staying there who were hanging out in the lobby.

"Thanks for the help on my homework, Maeve," said a girl named Olivia. "Amazing how much you know about quantum mechanics."

Max shrugged. "Just something I picked up."

"You're blooming brilliant, Maeve," the girl gushed. "A genius." (Maeve was the name Max had been using in the hostel. "M" aliases were always easier for her to remember.)

"Thanks," Max told her. "Anytime."

She headed down the corridor to her room.

When she unlocked the door and stepped inside, she

saw her roommate, Leo, crouched on the floor in front of the far wall.

He had his index finger stuck inside an electrical outlet. Again.

"Just using this temporary lull in our activity level to recharge my batteries," Leo explained when he saw Max rolling her eyes.

Leo was an automaton, or a human-like robot. A walking, talking mannequin with incredible AI (artificial intelligence) who looked like he just escaped from the boys' department of a clothing store. He had been designed to resemble a twelve-year-old male in order to make him seem less threatening.

Leo, formerly known as Lenard, was built by the Corp to be a tool in their hunt for Max Einstein. Fortunately, one of Max's colleagues at the Change Makers Institute, a sausage-loving kid from Poland named Klaus, was a robotics expert. After Max had captured Lenard, Klaus totally reprogrammed the bot's AI and turned him into the very helpful, very friendly Leo.

"He'll be the perfect roommate," Klaus had assured Max. "You have a question, he'll have an answer. And if he gets too chatty, you can always give him a swift kick in the butt to reboot him." Because Klaus was something of a jokester, he'd positioned the robot's reboot button on what people in London would call his "bum."

Fortunately, my fingers are outfitted with a universal adapter, allowing me to recharge in a type-G plug, the style typically found in the UK and Hong Kong. London, England is in the UK.
Hair never out of place, because it's plastic. It's also purplish.
Facial expressions totally lifelike and, therefore, creepy.
Eyes are high-definition cameras, so it can read human gestures and expressions.
Body consists of forty-four pneumatic joints.
Likes to hang out in the apartment without wearing any clothes.
Four feet, three inches tall.

"The temperature outside is thirteen degrees Celsius or fifty-five degrees Fahrenheit," said Leo, sounding like a supercharged Alexa or Siri. "It's mostly cloudy with sixty-seven percent humidity. Fog alerts are in effect for London, England, and the surrounding areas…"

"Thank you, Leo," said Max. "But I didn't ask for a weather report…"

"I do my best to anticipate your queries. The threat level is minimal. No Corp presence has been detected in our vicinity." And then, Leo giggled. He giggled a lot. It was a programming bug that even a robotics genius like Klaus couldn't erase from deep within the boy-bot's silicon chips.

"I'm going to go to bed," said Max. "Today was a rough one."

"Would you like to listen to music?" asked Leo. "I notice you are carrying a violin case. Perhaps you are in the mood for Bach's Concerto in D Minor for two violins? I could engage my synthesizer to provide the second violin…"

"No, thanks."

"Have you made your plans for tomorrow, Max? There are several more locations on your Einstein tour of London, England, list. If you would like to visit Waterloo Station, for instance, where Einstein was spotted during a July heat wave—looking cool in a thin white cotton jacket, a tennis shirt, and loose white trousers—I would suggest taking the

N38 bus, departing every five minutes, from Hyde Park Corner to Green Park Underground station where you would board the Jubilee line, also departing every five minutes, and disembark at Waterloo Station. I would not suggest wearing a tennis shirt as this is not a heat wave."

"Leo?"

"Yes?"

"You ever heard the expression TMI? Too much information?"

"Yes. One time when Klaus was cataloguing his wide variety of burps for me. He called that exercise 'TMI.'"

Max nodded. "Just try to remember what Einstein said: 'A theory is the more impressive the greater the simplicity of its premises.'"

"Understood. In the future, I will attempt to adhere to a protocol of simplicity in all things."

"Cool. Good night, Leo. See you in the morning."

"Sleep well, Max. As I mentioned earlier, the threat level from the Corp is currently at zero point five six nine percent. It is minimal."

Of course, what neither Leo nor Max could know was that, at that very hour, in a secret subterranean hideaway in West Virginia, a meeting was taking place.

Its goal?

To increase that threat level significantly.

# 5

The Corp's headquarters was hidden in a cavern, deep within the Appalachian mountains of West Virginia.

An emergency board meeting had been called.

"We have it on good authority that something big is coming from the young do-gooders at the Change Makers Institute," said the chairwoman, who, when she wasn't attending Corp board meetings, ran one of the world's largest entertainment conglomerates. In fact, all the members of the Corp board had very important positions at major corporations. Ringed around the massive oval table were representatives of big banking, big pharma, big oil, big media, big agriculture, and every other big industry in the world. The members of the board were united by one thing and one thing only: greed.

They wanted to make money. As much as possible. Because money bought access to power. Money wrote laws. Money could buy elections so, therefore, money could mold and shape the world the way the members of the Corp wanted it molded and shaped.

No politician dared oppose the Corp's will or might. No media outlet, either.

The only real threat to the Corp's dominance was a group of nerdy young geniuses, led by a twelve-year-old girl named Max Einstein, that was financed by a mysterious benefactor known only as "Ben."

"The CMI's do-gooder projects continue to interfere with our money-making plans!" protested a man in a business suit and cowboy boots. He slammed his Stetson hat down on the table to emphasize his disgust. "And I want Lenard back! Them little brats stole our robot. There should be a law against that."

"Not if the automaton was being deployed for what some might consider nefarious purposes," counseled one of the board's many lawyers. "They could claim self-defense."

"I don't care," shouted the man with the Texas accent. "I want Lenard back so we can melt him down and make candles out of his waxy head."

"Lenard's retrieval should, indeed, become a top priority," said a German banker on the board. "After all, we invested heavily in his creation and manufacture. We did not do it so the other side could utilize his incredible artificial intelligence for charity missions."

"And, might I remind you all," said the chairwoman, "we would still like to, how shall I put this, *convince* Max Einstein to come to work for us. The girl is a genius and could become the shortcut we've been seeking to ensure that we will be the first to market with a quantum computer."

"Do you still think Dr. Zimm is the one to bring her in?" asked a woman from Australia whose family owned multiple TV networks around the world. "Does he still have the skills and expertise we require?"

The chairwoman shook her head. "No. We have lost all confidence in Dr. Zimm. He has found Max on several occasions only to fail in capturing her. And it was Dr. Zimm who lost Lenard—not to mention our very profitable bottled water subsidiary in India. In short, it is time for Dr. Zimm to go."

"So who will head up the hunt for Max Einstein?"

"Me," said a giant of a man who'd just marched into the boardroom. He stood nearly seven feet tall in his chunky military boots, and his head was shaped like an enormous pineapple without any fringe up top. When he moved, he jingled and jangled—signaling that his long black coat was lined with concealed weaponry.

"Ladies and gentlemen," said the chairwoman, "allow me to introduce Professor Von Hinkle. You will find his résumé on your tablet computers."

The other board members tapped the tinted glass screens built into every place at the table. There were audible gasps of shock as the board members scrolled through Professor Von Hinkle's long list of horrible accomplishments.

"You did that?" said one. "The poisonous gas leak?"

Von Hinkle shrugged. "We needed to evacuate the area to make room for a nuclear reactor."

"The oil fires that opened up the desert to new drilling," said another. "That was you, too?"

Von Hinkle nodded. "But, no one could ever prove it."

"And the ash slurry spill?"

"Let's just say we gave Mother Nature and the mud a gentle shove in the right direction."

"This is all well and good, professor," said the man from Texas. "Very impressive credentials. But how does creating all this mayhem qualify you to snatch and grab Max Einstein, not to mention our hijacked robot?"

"Simple," said Von Hinkle. "I'm ruthless, brutal, and cruel. Some might call me inhuman. I am also very, very efficient. Trust me. I will get this job done. The little girl and the little boy-bot? They don't stand a chance."

**6**

The next morning, still bored, Max pulled on her big floppy sweater and went souvenir shopping.

She came home with an Albert Einstein bobblehead doll (it was on display in a shop, right next to a solar-powered Queen Elizabeth doing a dainty royal wave). She placed her newest piece of Einstein memorabilia inside the battered old suitcase that, when propped open, served as her curio cabinet wherever she roamed.

The antique piece of luggage (it had to be older than Max) had been with her as long as she could remember. It was filled with photographs, books, and figurines—all celebrating her hero.

The oldest photograph in her collection, the one that someone other than Max (she had no idea who) had

pasted inside the lid so long ago that its edges were brown, showed the great professor lost in thought. He had a bushy mustache and long, wispy hair. His hands were clasped together, almost as if in prayer. His eyes were gazing up toward infinity.

That photograph was Max's oldest memory. And since she never knew her parents, she found herself talking to the kindly, grandfatherly man inside her suitcase at bedtime when she lived in orphanages or foster care facilities. Her Dr. Einstein photo was a very good listener. As she grew older, Max became curious as to who the mystery man might be, and that's how her lifelong infatuation with all things Einstein began.

Max flicked Leo's On switch. Sometimes she powered him down at night so he'd be quiet for a few hours.

"Good morning, Maxine," said Leo. "You have a new appointment."

"What?"

"While you were out, Benjamin messaged me. I would have told you sooner, but, as you might recall, you shut me off for the night. That, of course, is not necessary. You can simply request that I enter my silent sleep mode as outlined in the PDF manual that Klaus—"

"What did Ben want?" Max cut the chatty bot off. Sometimes, he never stopped talking!

"He would like to have lunch with you today at the Blueprint Café, located at 28 Shad Thames, London, England. According to my research, this long-time favorite is famous for its floor-to-ceiling windows offering a stunning view of the Thames River and Tower Bridge."

"What time?" she asked.

"Noon. I think you might enjoy the line-caught cod with a zingy green herb crust. It is stunning. Summer on a plate."

Max really needed to talk to Klaus about some software updates for Leo.

At noon, when Max entered the Blueprint Café, it was easy to spot Ben. He was the only person in the whole restaurant. There weren't even any servers or cooks, just platters of food under domes filling the three tables surrounding Ben.

"I bought out the restaurant for today's lunch," he told her. "I prefer privacy whenever possible."

Max nodded.

"Isn't the view spectacular?" Ben asked, gesturing to the wall of windows framing bridges, barges, boats, and London's skyline.

"Fabulous," said Max. She turned back to Ben. "So, what's our next mission?"

"Wouldn't you like to eat something first? I ordered fish and chips, rump steak, fried polenta, cauliflower soup, an apple and blackberry crumble..."

"I'm not really hungry. Besides, the last time we met, you sort of put me off feasting like this. You were telling me about world hunger, remember?"

"Yes. I recall that conversation..."

"You said seven hundred and ninety-five million humans go hungry every day. That's about one in every nine people. Then you told me thirty-six million of those same people will die from hunger this year."

"You sure you don't want some, uh, crumble from the pudding menu?"

"No. And why do people in England call desserts pudding even when it's not pudding?"

Ben's eyes twinkled. "Because they always have?"

Max liked it when Ben's eyes twinkled. She wasn't exactly sure why. Sitting with him, she always got butterflies in her stomach, which was another reason she wasn't really hungry for fish and chips or a "pudding" that sounded more like pie.

"Listen, Max," Ben said, taking a sip of tea, which seemed to be the only thing he was having for lunch. "I know you're anxious for your next assignment, but it's not quite ready for you. There are still a few details that need to be, you know, ironed out."

"Then what am I supposed to do?"

"Be patient. And enjoy London. Just be careful." Ben snapped open his attaché case and removed a clasped envelope. He opened it and pulled out a glossy photograph that he slid across the table to Max. "We have to worry about this man."

Actually, the man looked more like a craggy giant in a long black coat. His pineapple of a head was humongous and propped on top of a thick stump of a neck. He looked like he could be a cousin to the villain Thanos from the Avengers movies.

"Who is he?" Max asked.

"Your new nemesis. Professor Viktor Von Hinkle."

# 7

**"What about Dr. Zimm?" Max asked.**

Ben shook his head and tucked the photograph of Professor Von Hinkle back into his briefcase. "Our sources inform us he has been recently replaced by this new, much more ruthless adversary."

In a way, Max was sorry to hear it. Yes, Dr. Zimm was dangerous and despicable. But he had also claimed to know where Max came from. It could've been a big fat lie but every time she and the evil doctor bumped into each other, he promised to tell her "everything you've ever wanted to know." Max would do almost anything to find out who her parents were. Who *she* was. But she couldn't trust Zimm enough to believe him.

"The Corp is still actively searching for you, Max," Ben

continued. "This Professor Von Hinkle has been tasked with, well, basically kidnapping you. My sources say he is ten times worse than Dr. Zimm. Ruthless, coldhearted, and determined. They say he's a maniac who operates like a machine. Speaking of machines, the Corp would be pleased if Professor Von Hinkle grabbed the 'traitorous' Leo, too. Something about melting him down and turning him into a candle."

"They still want me to engineer a quantum computer for them?"

Ben nodded. "There's that. And they also think that if they remove you from my team, it will stop us from doing what we're going to do next."

"Which is?"

"Still confidential."

"So, again, what am I supposed to do?"

"Staying in your room would be one option."

"Seriously? I'd go nuts."

"London isn't exactly safe, Max. This city has a massive web of security cameras. They're everywhere. The Corp could tap into them and easily find you using facial recognition software."

Max sighed. Ben was giving her his puppy dog eyes—silently pleading with her to play it safe. Her usual steely resolve sometimes melted when he did that.

Like now.

"Okay," she said. "Fine. I'll be patient. But I'm not hiding in my room with Leo. I'll stick to my 'Einstein in London' tour. Don't worry—I'll be careful and be on the lookout for any Corp thugs. I just wish there was somebody who could play tourist with me."

Ben smiled.

Uh-oh. Did he think Max was asking him out on some kind of date?

"Not that I mind being on my own." Max backpedaled as fast as she could. "I mean, I've been alone most of my life. Another few days or weeks or whatever won't matter."

"But what if you didn't have to be alone?" asked Ben, softly.

Someone new strode into the restaurant.

"What's the story, Max?" she said in a thick Irish brogue. "Cooee, lassie, is that fish and chips I'm smellin'?"

It was Max's friend Siobhan, a member of her CMI team. Siobhan had fiery red hair and a temper to match. She was also fearless and had helped Max stand up to some extremely bad actors (whom Siobhan called "brutal thugs") on the team's missions in Ireland and Africa.

Max jumped out of her chair and threw her arms around her friend. Ben stood up and stuffed his hands in his pants pockets.

"You should probably hug Ben, too," Siobhan said when they finally broke off their embrace. "He's the one who invited me to fly down from Dublin so you wouldn't have to traipse around London all alone. Go on, Max. Give him a hug…"

"That's okay," said Ben, sounding flustered.

He sat down quickly. Max mirrored his move.

Siobhan pulled out a chair to join them.

"So what's with these private lunches, you two?" Siobhan asked. "Are these, like, dates?"

"We were, uh, discussing plans," said Ben. "For the future."

Siobhan winked at him. "I reckon you were, Benjamin." She lifted a dome off a plate, spotted the fish and chips (chips were the British/Irish term for French fries), and popped a crisp spud into her mouth. The she started batting her eyes and gushing like a cheesy romance novel: "Your beautiful, lovely future…*together*."

# 8

**Ben made a big show of checking his watch.**

"Oh, my. Would you look at the time?" He still sounded flummoxed. "I'm late for my next meeting. Now you don't have to explore London alone, Max. You and Siobhan should enjoy yourselves. See all the sights. I've arranged a car. Leo will be your driver."

"Seriously?"

Ben nodded. "Klaus assures me that Leo can turn any vehicle into an autonomous automobile. He'll pick you up out front when you want to leave, just hit him up with a text. Enjoy your lunch. I ordered one of everything and double puddings."

Ben plucked up his attaché case, clutched the boxy

thing to his chest, and waddled out of the dining room like a nervous penguin searching for the nearest restroom.

Siobhan chuckled a little and pulled the plate of fish and chips closer so she could devour it.

"Sorry," she explained between bites. "I'm a wee bit famished. All they served were peanuts on the plane. And it was one of Ben's private jets, too!"

Max decided to eat something as well. It would be a shame to let the food Ben ordered go to waste, especially with all the starving people in the world. So, she started with the "pudding"—the apple and blackberry crumble.

"So, did your boyfriend give you a clue as to what we'll be tacklin' next?" Siobhan asked after she'd cleaned her plate.

"He's not my boyfriend," Max said defensively.

"Says you…"

Max tried to change the subject. "When I first arrived in London, after the water project in India, Ben hinted that our next assignment might be to find a cure for world hunger."

"Must be why he ordered so much food," cracked Siobhan. "Fixing world hunger? Phew. That's a mighty tall order, Max."

"I know. But those are the only kind Ben likes."

"Cheeky little billionaire, isn't he?"

As much as they joked about Ben, both Max and Siobhan were extremely proud to be members of his Change Makers Institute. They were among a handful of young geniuses that Ben and his team had handpicked to try to solve problems that grown-ups couldn't or wouldn't.

And, of course, they were also among the handful of young geniuses the Corp was trying to hunt down and destroy.

Max's mind drifted to her new nemesis. Professor Von Hinkle.

*Could he and his evil minions find her, Leo, and Siobhan in London?*

They might be able to—especially if they had some good security camera hackers on their team. And, with the kind of money the Corp had, they definitely did.

"Siobhan—you see that cluster of white metal boxes attached to that pole out there?" Max gestured toward the window. "Those are CCTV security cameras. There are five hundred thousand of them watching almost every inch of central London."

"Half a million?" said Siobhan, adding a whistle.

Max nodded. "The average Londoner is caught on camera three hundred times a day. A tourist seeing the sights, probably more."

"And you think those goons at the Corp might tap into those cameras and find us using facial recognition software?"

"The thought crossed my mind," said Max. "Right after Ben mentioned it as a possibility."

"So, what do we do?"

"Use our brains and defeat the cameras while we go check out London in our own private car with Leo as our driver."

"And how do we do that?"

"By making our first stop some place that sells pretty stickers for scrapbookers!"

"Seriously?"

"Yep. If we plaster them on our face, throw off the symmetry that the facial recognition software will be seeking, we should be safe. We might want to buy some hats and sunglasses, too."

"How about those Groucho glasses with the fake nose and mustache—like on the cover of that book, *I Funny*?" joked Siobhan.

"Perfect," said Max. "Even if they're tapping every single CCTV camera in London, the Corp will never recognize us!"

# 9

Professor Von Hinkle's thick-heeled boots clomped like horse hooves on the concrete floor as he circled his predecessor. Dr. Zacchaeus Zimm was seated for their interview in a straight-backed metal chair, his legs shackled by chains, his hands secured behind his back with plastic zip ties.

"This will be over once you tell me everything you know about Max Einstein," said Von Hinkle. His deep, resonant voice made small objects in the room rattle.

"Your logic is flawed, professor," said Zimm, whose humiliation at the hands of the Corp hadn't drained away any of his arrogance. "If I tell you what I know, I lose any and all negotiating power with my former employers. By the way, this might be a good time for you to ponder how the Corp might treat you when it's time for your 'early retirement package.'"

Von Hinkle went to a shiny aluminum case sitting atop a work table. He snapped open the latches and removed a black metallic ball, the size of a bird's egg.

"Are you familiar with the T-2 tracker drones our friends at Slingshot Surveillance developed?" Thin wings shot up from the sides of the small ball.

"Of course," sniffed Dr. Zimm.

"But, have you heard about the brand new T-3s?" He held the black orb closer to Zimm's face. "I helped them with the design. You see this array of stingers along its sides? Each one is actually a hypodermic needle. The body of the flying bot carries miniature vials of potent pharmaceutical agents. Some to subdue. Some to coax out the truth from a reluctant subject. One to kill."

Von Hinkle withdrew a slender remote from the left pocket of his long coat. The T-3 drone sprang to life and, hummingbird wings fluttering, hovered like a tiny helicopter over his hand.

"Guess which drug we'll be using today?" he said with a crooked smile.

Dr. Zimm suddenly lost ninety percent of his arrogance. "The lethal injection?"

"So dramatic," said Von Hinkle. "No, Zacchaeus, I thought we'd start with the truth serum."

He tapped the remote one more time and the drone flew from his hand to Dr. Zimm's right arm. It darted in and stabbed Dr. Zimm with one of its tiny needles. Drug delivered, it zipped back to the table to find its foam resting slot among the eleven other T-3 drones nestled in the case.

Two minutes later, Dr. Zimm was telling Professor Von Hinkle what he'd always promised to tell Max Einstein.

*Everything.*

"I first met Max Einstein when she was just a baby," he droned in a hypnotic monotone. "I was posing, for the Corp, as a visiting professor at Princeton University in New Jersey. They had tasked me with stealing as much intellectual property as I could from the school. Max simply appeared one day in the basement of the house I had rented for my stay. The housekeeper found her crawling around on the floor near an antique suitcase with nothing in it but a photo of Albert Einstein and the cover sheet to an antique research paper entitled 'The Maximum Application of Einstein's Theory of General Relativity.' That's why I named her Max Einstein."

"Did you search for her parents?"

"Yes, though of course I did not involve the police. For several weeks, I hired nannies and nurses to look after her.

All reported that the child seemed to possess unusual talents and skills. She was remarkably advanced for her age."

"Go on," said Professor Von Hinkle. "What happened next?"

"Sensing that the child was special, it was decided that I should immediately transport her to an 'undercover Christmas tree farm,' a safe house that the Corp maintained outside Elkins, West Virginia."

"Did her parents ever enter the picture? Were they searching for her?"

Dr. Zimm shook his head. "She was abandoned. An orphan. We ran several tests at the safe house and realized immediately that she possessed a genius IQ. Unfortunately, within a year, a soft-hearted psychologist, a Dr. Victoria Bartlett, didn't like us treating the child as if she were, as she put it, 'a lab rat.' She snatched the infant away and put her some place where 'we would never find her.'"

"And did the Corp find Dr. Bartlett?"

"Yes. We captured her outside Poughkeepsie. She was transferred to our re-education facility in northern Greenland."

"Is that so?"

Dr. Zimm nodded and his heavy chin slumped to his chest. Drool dribbled out of the corner of his mouth. The truth drug had made him drowsy.

"Go ahead, Zacchaeus," Von Hinkle said, his voice eerily soothing. "Sleep. And when you wake up, don't be surprised if you find yourself in northern Greenland. Maybe you'll even be reunited with Dr. Bartlett!"

There was a knock on the interview room's steel door.

"Enter," said Von Hinkle.

One of his assistants stepped into the room. "Sorry to disturb you, professor."

"I trust this is urgent?"

"Yes, professor. We have a hit. A college student has identified Max Einstein. She's staying at a youth hostel in London."

Von Hinkle snapped shut the lid on his collection of high-tech flying gizmos. He had to smile. His low-tech idea of placing "missing person" ads featuring Max Einstein's photograph in college papers across the globe had paid off first.

"Kindly instruct the good Samaritan who found our 'missing daughter' to not let her out of their sight. And, Matthew?"

"Sir?"

"Scramble a snatch-and-grab team in London. Immediately!"

# 10

"You need to pack your things, ladies," said Leo bright and early the next morning. "The benefactor has summoned the entire CMI team to Oxford. You will not be returning to London."

Max and Siobhan rubbed the sleep out of their eyes.

"Do you know what time it is, Leo?" said Max.

"It is currently six fifteen a.m. in London, England. I have prepared a pot of English breakfast tea as it seemed appropriate for morning consumption. There is a train to Oxford from London, England's Paddington Station departing at seven seventeen, seven thirty-one, seven forty-three..."

"We get it," said Siobhan. "There's a lot of bloomin' trains from London to Oxford."

"Seventy-seven per day," said Leo. "Average journey time varies from fifty-one minutes to one hour and fourteen minutes."

"Is Ben ready to reveal our next big project?" asked Max.

"His encrypted message was not specific in that regard," said Leo. "However, logic dictates that, if we will not be returning to London, England, we must be moving on from Oxford to somewhere new. The likely supposition would be our next project."

Leo's use of the words *we* and *our* made Max grin. Only a month ago, he was working for the enemy, helping the Corp track Max and sabotage the CMI's efforts.

"Power down to sleep mode," Max told him. "We need to put you back in the rolling box."

"Oh, joy," said Leo. Then, after hiccupping a burst of giggles, he shut himself down.

Neither Siobhan nor Max traveled with a lot of baggage. Max had her Einstein memorabilia suitcase and a duffel bag. Siobhan had all her things stuffed inside a backpack. They put Leo into the rolling steamer trunk that Klaus had designed for the boy-bot's transportation needs, then they headed out into the hall.

Olivia, the friendly college student Max (or Maeve) had helped with her quantum physics homework, was in the lobby, pretending to check her mailbox. Max knew she was pretending because the mail was typically delivered late in the afternoon.

"Where are you going so early, Max?" Olivia said. "Or should I still pretend to call you *Maeve?*"

"Excuse me?" said Max.

"Your parents are very worried about you, Max. They placed an ad in the *Imperial College* newspaper. It had your picture and everything."

"Let me guess," said Siobhan. "Did Max's parents offer a reward?"

"Why, yes. Ten thousand pounds. But that's not the reason I called the number. They miss you, Max. They're sending someone over to collect you in fifteen minutes."

"Too bad she won't be here," said Siobhan. "Come on, Max. We have a plane to catch."

"Where do you think you're going?" demanded Olivia.

"Rome," said Max. "I hear the pasta is fantastic."

"Step aside, lassie," said Siobhan, barreling ahead with the rolling steamer trunk, using it like a snowplow to clear the corridor.

"I'm going to tell them where you're headed!" Olivia shouted after them as they trundled the trunk down the stoop steps and bolted into the street.

"Rome is a big place!" Max replied. "They'll never find us."

Siobhan hailed a cab. They loaded up their luggage and headed off to Paddington Station.

"Smart telling Olivia we had a plane to catch," Max told Siobhan when they were underway.

"I know. That's why I'm with the CMI, Max. I'm a bloomin' genius."

While the cab ferried them to Paddington Station, Max and Siobhan plastered more stickers on their faces to, once again, fool the CCTV security cameras. When they arrived at the station, they purchased tickets (from a machine to avoid human interaction and someone remembering their stickered faces) and quickly found seats on the next train to Oxford. Leo was riding in the overhead luggage rack. At 7:17 a.m. on the dot, they pulled out of Paddington.

"Right on time," said Siobhan.

Max nodded. "And now I really wish I had a time machine."

"What for?"

"To go back to when I first met Olivia so I could completely ignore her. What was I thinking? Why did I try to make friends with the college kids? I should've remained invisible."

"Ah, that's no way to live, Max. You can't let the Corp turn you into a hermit, always looking for your next hidey-hole."

"I guess…"

"So, do you think time travel is actually possible?"

Max nodded. "Yes."

"Why?"

"Because Dr. Einstein did."

# 11

Max felt confident that their "Rome ruse" (as Siobhan started calling it) had sent the Corp henchmen scurrying off to Heathrow International Airport to nab her. So being on a train, she relaxed enough to re-create her hero's famous light-clock thought experiment about time travel for Siobhan.

"There are all kinds of clocks," Max told her friend as the train clacked along the tracks, heading north to Oxford, home of the famous university. "Most of them measure how many times a repetitive action is carried out. A regular tick-tock kind of rhythm. In theory, we could use light to make a clock, too."

"How?" said Siobhan. "One of those digital clocks that project the time on the ceiling?"

"No. I'm talking about bouncing a pulse of light between two mirrors that are a known distance apart."

"How do you make the light bounce? Is it made out of rubber?"

Max grimaced at her friend's bad joke. "It's a thought experiment, Siobhan. One of Albert Einstein's most famous. You just have to imagine it."

"Okay. I'm closing my eyes. I'm seeing the bouncing ball of light. It's hitting the mirrors…"

"Great. There's a regular beat to the bounce…"

"Definitely. You could dance to it." Siobhan started tapping her foot to the imaginary beat.

"Okay. Now let's put our light clock on this train with us. It's just ticking away, right?"

"Right. I'm watching the ball bounce up and down, up and down…"

"Now I'm holding the light clock up to the window."

Siobhan gave Max a strange look. "Why?"

"So people outside can see it," Max explained.

"Very considerate."

"Keep your eyes shut."

Siobhan obeyed. "I am."

"And let's say the train accelerates to half the speed of light."

"Crikey. It better not. I might toss my cookies…"

Max said patiently, "Use your imagination."

"Okay. We're really whizzing along now."

"This is an express train, so it'll skip the next station. But there's a guy standing on the platform."

"What's his name?"

Max rolled her eyes. "Doesn't matter."

Siobhan grinned. "Maybe not to you, Max, but it would to him."

She took a deep breath. "Fine. Let's call him Bob. Bob is standing on the platform as we fly by and he sees my clock in the window. But he doesn't see it the way we do. Instead of a ball of light bouncing up and down in a straight line, Bob would see the light mapping out a series of triangles."

"Does Bob know trigonometry?" asked Siobhan. "The study of triangles?"

"Indeed he does. Very bright guy, our friend Bob."

"So," said Siobhan, who was as much of a math whiz as Max, "he does a mess of Pythagorean theorem calculations on those right triangles streaking past him and figures out the length of their diagonal hypotenuses and, uh-oh, he's measuring time differently than you and me on the fast-flying train. Time is moving slower to him."

"Exactly. For us, time is passing normally. For him, it's slowed down. So, that's the paradox. Time flows at different rates relative to movement: a moving light clock will

A.

B.

always look like it's running slow to someone in a stationary position. That's why we need to factor in Einstein's theory of relativity and time dilation to make the whole GPS system work. All that hands-free navigation depends on very accurate clocks zooming around the globe in fast-moving satellites. Nobody would be able to find what they're looking for on their map apps if we ignored what Einstein taught us about a moving clock slowing."

"So if we stay on this imaginary, half-the-speed-of-light bullet train for a long enough time, with our clock slowing down in Bob's world, we could end up in Bob's future, right?"

"Correct."

"One last question."

"Go on?"

"Will Bob have a better haircut in the future because, honestly, from what I saw in my imagination, I think his mum just plops a bowl on top of his head and cuts around the rim..."

The two friends were laughing so hard, they nearly forgot to get off the train at Oxford Station.

But then someone started banging a fist against their window.

# 12

"Where's Leo?" came the muffled cry of a very agitated Klaus from the other side of the glass. "Why isn't he riding with you guys?"

Her heart thumping wildly from the sudden noise, Max gestured to the overhead luggage rack.

"You made him ride all the way from London in his box?" Klaus sounded horrified. "Monsters!"

The blustery Klaus—who, at one point, wanted to take over Max's role as CMI team leader—had mellowed ever since they'd taken the robot Lenard from the Corp. His entire focus had shifted to making technological magic with his amazing new electronic toy that he renamed Leo.

Max and Siobhan quickly pulled down the boy-bot's rolling travel box, grabbed their things, and hurried off the

65

train. Klaus immediately opened Leo's box to make sure he "hadn't suffocated" on the ride, even though robots don't breathe.

Charl and Isabl, the security team charged with protecting the CMI field team, were on the platform, too. Neither Charl nor Isabl had a last name that they cared to share with anyone, but they were both very skilled in the martial arts and the use of tactical weapons. They were like a two-person commando unit.

"I trust your journey was unremarkable?" said Charl with his hard-to-place, somewhere-in-Eastern-Europe accent.

Max nodded. "Once we got on the train."

"Max's cover was blown in London," said Siobhan.

"We know," said Isabl. Her accent was slightly more exotic than Charl's.

"The Corp might be under the impression I'm on my way to Rome," said Max with a smirk.

Charl nodded. "They sent a two-member strike team to Heathrow. Caused a bit of a row. They also alerted their assets in Italy."

"Good," said Siobhan. "Just so long as they don't know we're here."

"They don't," said Isabl. "You two can peel those stickers off your faces now."

"Oh, right," said Siobhan. "Duh."

"All threats within the confines of the United Kingdom have been neutralized," said Leo. Klaus had hauled him out of his box and powered him up.

"Let's go," said Charl. "We have an electric-powered SUV."

"And Leo is *not* being stowed in the rear cargo area," said Klaus. He gave Max and Siobhan a squinty eyed look of disgust. "Animals."

The city of Oxford, fifty-one miles outside of London, was home to what was probably the most famous university in the whole world. Its first colleges opened more than eight hundred years ago inside medieval buildings that looked like castles and cathedrals, causing one poet to call Oxford the "City of Dreaming Spires."

Isabl was behind the wheel of the SUV. She was a very skilled driver. In fact, she was so good, she could've been a stunt driver in the Fast and Furious movies.

As they drove through the awe-inspiring city, goose bumps sprung up on Max's arms. Not because of all the incredible architecture but because she realized she was in another space where Albert Einstein had visited at a different time. He gave a series of lectures at the renowned university in the early 1930s. The deans and dons of the college were so impressed that they kept the blackboard he used during his lectures, along with all his chalk notes. It

Real Cathedral of
Higher Learning

The word *snob* originated in
Oxford as an abbreviation of
the Latin phrase *sine nobilitate,*
which means "without nobility."
Glad Siobhan, Isabl, and
I came to Oxford after
1878. Before that, no girls
were allowed.

Home, origin, and birthplace
of the Oxford comma.

was now on display at the university's Museum of the History of Science. Max hoped there'd be time in her schedule to go see it.

The SUV pulled up in front of a building that looked more like a medieval monastery than a dormitory.

"This is home for a few days," said Charl. "Everybody out."

Klaus tapped Max on the shoulder before she could climb out. "You should take better care of Leo," he whispered when the others were out on the sidewalk. "He knows things."

Max arched a curious eyebrow.

"After we freed Lenard from the Corp," Klaus whispered, "I didn't completely scrub his artificial intelligence. I left in the stuff Dr. Zimm taught him about you."

# 13

Charl and Isabl stayed outside with Leo and Klaus as Max and Siobhan made their way into the dorm lobby.

Max wished Leo was with her. She wanted to immediately download whatever facts about her childhood Klaus had discovered and left stored inside the robot's memory. Now she was worried that Klaus would claim Leo as *his* roommate.

"Hey, Max! What's up, Siobhan?"

Keeto, a brilliant young computer scientist from Oakland, California was the first Change Maker to greet them in the fusty lobby of the dormitory. Keeto had grown up on the other side of the Bay Bridge from Silicon Valley. That was like living in New Jersey and staring at the skyscrapers of New York. It just made you feel like you had something to prove. Keeto had a computer-sized chip on his shoulder and told everybody who would listen that he was destined to become "the next Steve Jobs."

"Hey, Keeto," said Max. "Great to see you."

"Yeah," said the cocky Keeto. "I get that a lot."

"Where's everybody else?" asked Siobhan.

"In the study room I've organized," replied the stern voice of a middle-aged woman who'd just stepped into the lobby. It was Ms. Tari Kaplan, the no-nonsense "house mother" from the first Change Maker gathering in Jerusalem.

"What are they doing in a bloomin' study room?" asked Siobhan.

"Studying," replied Ms. Kaplan, drily.

"For what?" asked Max. "Did Ben tell them our next assignment?"

"No," said Ms. Kaplan. "They are simply using their time wisely."

"Well, let's go say hello," said Max. "I can't wait to lead everybody on our next assignment."

"Too right," said Siobhan. "We're gonna save the world...again!"

"Boo-yah!" shouted Keeto.

Ms. Kaplan shook her head. "Your youthful idealism is, I suppose, commendable. However, it is not enough.

Idealism soon withers in the harsh light of experience. It is inevitably crushed by time and reality. You will see."

"Whoa," said Keeto. "Anybody ever tell you you're a real downer, Ms. K?"

"No. They tell me I'm a realist. Because that's what I am. Come along, you three. The others are already ahead of you."

"Ahead of us?" said Siobhan.

"Yes. They have a head start on their test prep."

"Test?" said Max, who, much like her idol, Albert Einstein, hated tests. Einstein wasn't big on cramming facts into his brain, figuring he could always look those up in a book. No, he thought education should be about training the mind to think. Max totally agreed.

"Come along, Maxine," said Ms. Kaplan. "I won't have you slowing us down. Again."

*Again?* thought Max. *When had she ever slowed down the CMI team?*

Maybe the first time they all took tests. She even walked out on one exam.

"Ms. Kaplan," said Siobhan. "Max is our leader. The chosen one. Because Ben *chose* her. Remember?"

"For the first two assignments," said Ms. Kaplan, still moving swiftly down the musty corridor. "However, she may not have what it takes to lead us into the future."

"Oh, snap," said Keeto. "That was so shady, I just got chilly."

Finally, Ms. Kaplan stopped in her tracks and turned around.

"No, Keeto, that is not 'shady.' It is simply a realistic assessment of our situation. And, as I said, I am a realist. You three would be wise to become the same!"

# 14

**Max really didn't care about being "the chosen one"** or the big cheese in charge.

She just wanted to do good in the world.

So did all the other members of the team, except maybe Ms. Kaplan. She seemed to be hung up on titles and power trips.

*Stay away from negative people, Max,* urged the gentle Einstein inside her head. *Remember—they always have a problem for every solution. Keep away from people who belittle your ambitions.*

*Sometimes I can't,* she silently told her inner Einstein. *Sometimes they're the ones in charge!*

Ms. Kaplan led the way into a room with a high vaulted ceiling. The walls were paneled in dark wood. Some of the

windows featured stately stained glass. Dusty oil portraits of great minds and honored professors, all in gilt-edge frames, were everywhere. For an instant, Max thought she had been transported to Hogwarts.

The other members of Max's Change Makers team were seated at long library tables, poring over stacks of books.

Max smiled as she glanced around the stuffy room. Her teammates were all brilliant. This was like a reunion of the Genius Avengers.

Her friend from Ireland, Siobhan, was an expert in geoscience. That meant she knew the earth and its secrets. Siobhan's goal? To help save lives by one day being able to accurately predict catastrophic events such as earthquakes, hurricanes, and floods.

Keeto was a computer science geek (his term). There was no code he couldn't crunch or crack.

Toma, from China, was a budding astrophysicist who shared Max's fascination with Einstein's theories about black holes. Toma was also big on "dark matter" and wormholes. He usually dressed in T-shirts blasting intergalactic messages. Today's simply said, "Space Nerd."

Hana, from Japan, was a botanist, totally obsessed with plants. She was a vegan and thought the planet would be much better off if everybody followed a plant-based diet.

You did not want to get her started about beef cows and methane gas.

Then there was Tisa. A biochemist from Kenya who hated tests just as much as Max did. Maybe that's why they'd become such good friends. Tisa also made sure everybody knew that even though her father was one of the wealthiest industrialists in all of Africa, this had absolutely nothing to do with her being chosen for the CMI team. "Ben doesn't need my father's money," she'd say. "He has enough of his own."

Annika, from Germany, was a master of formal logic, which she considered to be a science right up there with chemistry, biology, and astrophysics. "Without logic," she'd argue, "none of those other sciences could function."

Vihaan, whose home was in India, had university degrees in quantum mechanics even though he was only thirteen. But he wasn't in Oxford because he was needed back home, overseeing the team's extremely successful water purification project. Despite the best efforts from the Corp to sabotage their plans, Vihaan's community now had access to clean water, something many people took for granted.

When Toma, Hana, Tisa, and Annika (Max wondered if there was something to geniuses having an "A" at the end of their names) looked up from their studies and saw Max, they cheered.

Klaus and Leo strode into the room behind her.

"That's right," said Klaus, pretending the applause and cheers were for him. "I'm here. Leo, too. It's time to get this party started!"

"This is not a party, Klaus," snapped Ms. Kaplan. "This is a deadly serious endeavor."

"Doesn't mean we have to be deadly serious, now, does it?" said Tisa with her sunny smile. "Just sayin', Ms. K."

"Just because we are smart," added Annika, "does not, ipso facto, mean we need to be glum."

"So, let's get busy," said Keeto. "What's the next global problem we're gonna slay?"

"World hunger," said a voice broadcasting out of a miniature Bluetooth speaker Charl had just brought into the room.

It was Ben!

Max grinned. This was real. It was officially time to go back to work.

And Max couldn't wait to get started.

Right *after* she learned everything Leo knew about her past.

# 15

"Welcome to, uh, Oxford." Ben's voice rang out from the speaker. "I've brought you all together here because Sir Gordon Richards, one of the world's foremost experts on the global food crisis, will be giving a series of lectures at Rhodes House, which is here in Oxford."

For a nanosecond, Max forgot all about Leo and the secrets buried in his memory chips.

Rhodes House on South Parks Road in Oxford was where Albert Einstein lectured in May 1931. He talked about the density of matter in the universe. (Too bad Toma hadn't been there to hear that lecture.) Professor Einstein was also given an honorary Doctor of Science degree by the university. Rhodes House was another space that Max wished she could visit about ninety years ago.

"Ms. Kaplan will tell you the details," Ben's voice continued. "I just, you know, wanted to say, uh, 'Welcome to Oxford,' which I already did and, you know, wish you guys luck. If anyone can solve the world hunger problem, I hope it's you! So, like I said, good luck! Tari? The floor is yours. Not literally. It belongs to Oxford, so..."

The speaker went silent for a second.

"Never mind," said Ben, who obviously hated speaking in public, even when nobody could see him. "As always, if you need any resources or, you know, money—just give me a call."

And, with a click, he was gone.

Ms. Kaplan strode to the front of the room.

"You should take notes," she announced. "This will be included on the final exam."

"Exam?" Tisa said what Max was thinking.

"Yes, Tisa. You heard correctly. We will be conducting a new battery of tests and examinations to determine who among you will be the new project leader. This world hunger task is so monumental it might require different talents than those utilized thus far."

In other words, Ms. Kaplan didn't think Max should be the "chosen one" anymore.

Ms. Kaplan clicked a remote and the projected image of a very proper-looking English gentleman filled a blank space on a white wall.

"Meet Sir Gordon Richards, the world's premier thinker on the global hunger crisis. In his lectures, Sir Richards will examine the very serious issues critical to our global food supply, from the science of agricultural advances to the politics of food security. He will also outline a plan for ending hunger that is sustainable and achievable."

"And then we'll come up with something better," cracked Keeto.

"Perhaps, Keeto," said Ms. Kaplan through a nasty squint. "However, we all have much we can learn from Sir Richards. Even a so-called genius such as yourself. Our hope is that the lectures will stimulate new ideas, new thinking. And, even more important, new leadership for this team."

*Wow,* thought Max. *She seriously wants to demote me.*

Max boldly raised her hand.

"Yes, Ms. Einstein?" said Ms. Kaplan. Actually, she kind of sneered it. "Do you have a question?"

"Yeah. When are the lectures?"

"Tomorrow. The first one will commence at eight a.m. sharp."

"Great. Thanks." That meant Max had all night to find out what Leo knew about who she was.

Provided, of course, that Klaus would let her have a few hours alone with his prized robot.

# 16

"You had her in London and you let her slip away?" demanded the chairwoman.

She pounded her fists on the table, rattling all the crystal water goblets lined up in front of the scowling billionaires.

Professor Von Hinkle smirked. This was his first "dressing down" at the hands of the Corp's board of directors. He was enjoying it. The so-called power brokers ringing the enormous table were imbeciles. They didn't appreciate his genius.

Not yet anyway.

"Dadgumit, son," snarled the Texan, "you're worse than that Dr. Zimm feller. That pair of British assassins you hired fell for that old 'I'm goin' out to the airport to catch a plane to Rome' bit? Shoot, son—that one's as old as

Moses. Why didn't your boys in London use some kind of tracking device or tap into all them security cameras they got over there?"

Professor Von Hinkle waited patiently as the angry Texan's ear tips went from red to pink and finally to a fleshy white. "Are you quite finished?" he asked, nonchalantly.

"I reckon," said the Texan.

"Good. Then allow me to bring you ladies and gentlemen up to speed. We didn't 'lose' Max in London. We merely flushed her out of her hiding place. Much as one flushes birds out of the bushes before pelting them with a shotgun blast. Movement puts your target in play. We now know with one hundred percent certainty that Max Einstein and the majority of her CMI compatriots have gathered at Oxford."

"That the fancy school in England?" asked the Texan.

"Yes," replied Von Hinkle.

"How did you come across this information?" asked the board chairwoman.

"The old-fashioned way. No surveillance cameras. No satellite imagery. No tracking devices. Just reliable human intelligence."

"You have an asset on the ground?"

Von Hinkle nodded. "Indeed I do."

"Who is it?" demanded the chairwoman.

Another smirk from Von Hinkle. "Sorry, ma'am. That information is confidential."

"What's the little girl's security situation?" asked the Texan. "She got much protection?"

"Hardly," scoffed Von Hinkle. "There are two commando types guarding Max and the other children. Their names are Charl and Isabl."

"Last names?" asked another board member.

Von Hinkle shook his head. "They prefer not to use those. I suspect Charl and Isabl are pseudonyms."

"Huh?" grunted the Texan.

"They're fake names. There is another adult with the young do-gooders. A foul-tempered instructor from the Change Makers Institute in Jerusalem, a middle-aged woman named Tari Kaplan. But, she is in no way a threat. She is merely a teacher."

"What about our dadgurn robot? Is he over there in Oxford, too?"

Von Hinkle nodded.

"Then what are you waiting for? Haul your butt on over to England! Go grab Max Einstein and Lenard."

"You may borrow the SST," said the chairwoman.

Von Hinkle smirked again. He knew they'd give him the SST.

SST was short for Supersonic Transport. Jets that could

fly faster than the speed of sound. Even though the Concorde (the only commercial SST) was banned from the skies years ago because of its ozone-searing exhaust fumes as well as its window-rattling sonic booms, the Corp still maintained its own secret SST. It flew at 2.2 times the speed of sound and could make the trip from West Virginia to London in a little over three hours.

"Thank you for the use of your jet," said Von Hinkle, bowing slightly at the waist. "It will surely speed up my delivery time."

"But don't y'all dare come back without Max Einstein!" screamed the Texan. "Or our dadgum robot."

"Rest assured we won't."

The Corp's supersonic private jet could seat eight. That's all the professor needed. There would be plenty of room for him *and* the seven heavily armed mercenaries on his snatch-and-grab team. The ones who were willing to complete missions at any cost.

Max and Lenard wouldn't know what hit them.

# 17

Before Max could check into her dorm room and find out what Leo knew, she and the others—along with Charl and Isabl—were escorted into a dining hall for what Ms. Kaplan called a "world hunger banquet."

There were three tables set up inside the dining hall. One had very nice plates, crystal stemware, and a fine linen tablecloth with a pretty centerpiece of purple roses. The second table was set for two people with disposable plastic cups, plastic spoons, and paper plates. The third table had no chairs and no actual place settings—just a stack of plastic cups and a pile of paper plates piled up in the middle. There was garbage, flattened cardboard boxes, and empty cans scattered around on the floor near the third table.

"Looks like a bloomin' trash heap," Siobhan whispered to Max.

"Welcome to the hunger banquet," said Ms. Kaplan. "Before we eat, let's take a quick quiz."

Max glanced at Tisa. Both of them rolled their eyes. Ms. Kaplan definitely loved giving quizzes and exams.

"True or false," Ms. Kaplan continued. "Overpopulation is the main cause of hunger."

"True!" blurted Klaus, who always wanted to be the smartest boy in any class.

"False. The world produces enough grain to feed every single human being on the planet thirty-five hundred calories a day. That's enough excess calories to make most of us fat."

Klaus, who was slightly pudgy, looked down at his shoes.

"True or false," said Ms. Kaplan. "Hunger affects the young and old, men and women, boys and girls equally."

"False!" said Keeto.

"Correct," said Ms. Kaplan. "The vast majority of the people who die because of hunger are boys and girls under the age of five, the elderly, and women."

As Ms. Kaplan ran through a few more true/false questions, Max realized what an enormous task this new project would be. Solving world hunger was going to be way more difficult than finding a solution for clean water in India or cheap electricity in a remote African village.

"Now, then," said Ms. Kaplan, "let us pretend that the ten of us represent the world's population. Ten percent of us would live in a rich country."

"That means just one of us," said Annika.

"Exactly. Annika, please take your seat at the rich table." Ms. Kaplan gestured to the fancy table with the flowers and fine china. "You will be enjoying a full meal with meat, fresh vegetables, some lovely roasted potatoes, a glass of milk, and cake for dessert."

Annika sat down, alone. A waiter came into the dining hall with a domed plate. Whatever was underneath the silver lid smelled delicious.

"Would you like your milk now," the waiter asked, "or with dessert?"

"With the cake," said Annika, sounding excited.

"But of course." The waiter bowed and departed.

Ms. Kaplan addressed the rest of the group: "Twenty percent of you live in middle-class countries."

"That's just two of us," said Toma.

"Correct. Charl and Isabl? Congratulations. You have worked hard and have enough food to meet your needs. Tonight, you will be dining on rice and beans. You will also be drinking clean water."

"That's okay," said Charl. "We don't need rice *and* beans."

"Two of the kids should sit at the middle-class table," added Isabl.

Ms. Kaplan shook her head. "No. I insist."

Charl and Isabl sat down. The waiter came back with a pot of rice, a steaming bowl of cooked black beans, and a pitcher of clear water.

"That leaves the rest of us." Ms. Kaplan pointed to the table with the stack of disposable cups and plates for a centerpiece. "We will represent the seventy percent of the world's population that is poor. We do not have enough food. We do not have access to clean water. Every day, we must make hard choices about who will eat and how much. Tonight, the seven of us will share a small pot of rice and some water from a well in our village."

"Where are our chairs?" asked Keeto.

"And utensils," Klaus whined.

"We cannot afford luxuries such as chairs," said Ms. Kaplan. "We will sit on the floor and eat with our hands."

"Um, there's garbage all over the floor," said Tisa.

"Yes," said Ms. Kaplan. "There is."

Now the waiter walked in with a small pot of rice and a jug of murky brown liquid that looked disgusting. *Like the water in Vihaan's grandfather's village before we came up with a solution,* thought Max.

"Ah, here comes our rice and water. Unfortunately, it is dirty water."

Klaus raised his hand.

"Yes?"

"Was the rice cooked in the dirty water?"

Ms. Kaplan nodded.

"Great..."

"Please, poor people," said Ms. Kaplan. "Join me. Find a seat on the floor. We will divide up the rice. Decide who gets more, who gets less. And remember—seventy percent of the earth's population must make this same choice every single day of their lives."

Max and Siobhan squatted on the floor with the others. Ms. Kaplan served up meager portions of the rice in paper bowls. Nobody was thirsty for the water. Nobody was hungry for the rice, either.

"Tomorrow," Siobhan whispered to Max, "you and I are splitting a whole supreme pizza. For breakfast!"

# 18

When the world hunger banquet was over, Ms. Kaplan made a small speech hoping everyone learned something from their dining (or lack of dining) experience.

"Yeah," said Keeto. "I learned my stomach really grumbles and gurgles when it's empty."

Everybody laughed. Except Annika. She was busy licking the last bit of frosting off her cake fork. (She'd had different forks for all the different courses of her rich country meal.)

"You guys are dismissed until tomorrow morning's lecture," said Charl.

When he said that, Klaus bolted out of the room.

"Crikey," said Siobhan. "Where's he going in such a hurry?"

"I suspect he's calling in an urgent pizza order," muttered Keeto.

"Come on," Max said to Siobhan. "He needs to let us borrow Leo."

The two friends took off running.

"Max!" shouted Isabl. "Go to your room. No late-night strolls while we're here in Oxford. Siobhan, take Max to your room immediately."

"I will," said Siobhan. "Just as soon as we have Leo!"

Siobhan and Max followed Klaus down a corridor. He ducked right and headed down some steps. So Siobhan and Max took a right and headed down the steps, too.

"Klaus?" they shouted. "Klaus!"

"What?"

At the foot of the steps, Klaus was standing in a pool of bright, fluorescent light, digging in his pockets for something. He looked surprised to see them.

Max slowed down, suddenly cautious.

What was Klaus up to? Could he be doing something nefarious? Something that involved the Corp?

Siobhan and Max made it to the bottom and saw the source of the strange light. Max giggled at her own suspicions. The light was beaming out of a vending machine loaded with candy bars and bags of what the English called crisps and Americans called potato chips.

"Do either of you have fifty pence?" Klaus asked, his hands jammed deep inside his pants pockets.

"Depends," said Siobhan. "Are you going to let Max borrow Leo tonight?"

"Yes. *If* she has 50p."

Max dug into her pocket and found a fifty pence coin.

Klaus got his Aero candy bar.

Max got Leo.

"Good to see you again, Max," said Leo after he was powered up inside Siobhan and Max's dorm room.

"Good to see you, too, Leo," said Max.

Suddenly, the glass in the windows rattled.

"Crikey," said Siobhan. "What the heck was that?"

"Sounded and felt like a sonic boom," said Max.

"Agreed," said Leo.

"There must be a military airbase close by."

"I can check that for you," offered Leo.

"Not right now," said Max. "We have more important matters to discuss."

"Reckon I'll give you two some privacy," said Siobhan, pouring a fistful of coins out of a small change purse. "All of a sudden, I fancy some Tayto cheese-and-onion crisps. Maybe a Kit Kat bar. Saw both in that vending machine downstairs. Ta!"

She left the room. Leo and Max were alone.

Max got right to the point. No use beating around the bush with a machine. "So how come you never mentioned what Dr. Zimm told you about me?"

"I don't recall you ever requesting that specific information, Maxine." Leo closed his eyes. Max could hear his hard drive whirring. "Checking. Checking. Confirmed. I have scrolled through the complete catalogue of our mutual dialogues. That question was never posed."

Max let out an exasperated breath. *Robots.* "Okay. I'm asking now. What do you know about who I am or where I came from?"

"Only what Dr. Zimm downloaded into my memory chips."

"Which is?"

"You were, twelve years ago, a baby."

Max rolled her eyes. Sometimes, conversing with the automaton could be extremely frustrating.

"Of course I was a baby twelve years ago," she snapped. "That's when I was born."

"We can assume that is correct."

"Huh?"

"Dr. Zimm discovered you when you were not yet speaking. You were, however, crawling across the floor of his basement laboratory. Therefore, he postulates that you were between seven and ten months old."

"Wait a second. I was crawling around on the floor of Dr. Zimm's lab?"

"Affirmative."

"Where was this lab?"

"In a basement."

"Where was the basement? And, I promise you, Leo, if you say, 'underneath a house,' I'm going to scream."

"The basement was situated in a place called Princeton, New Jersey. Not far from the university where Dr. Zimm was doing intellectual espionage work for the Corp."

"I'm from New Jersey?" said Max.

"So it would seem."

"Who were my parents?"

"Unknown."

"What did Dr. Zimm tell you about them?"

"That he never located your birth parents. He did, however, find your suitcase."

"Excuse me?"

Leo gestured toward Max's propped-open Einstein shrine.

"Your suitcase. When Dr. Zimm first saw it, twelve years ago, it was not as cluttered as it is currently. Twelve years ago, there was only one photograph of Dr. Einstein taped inside. It was accompanied by the cover sheet to a scholarly paper titled 'The Maximum Application of Einstein's Theory of General Relativity.'"

"Who wrote the paper?"

"I'm sorry, I do not have that information."

"Were my parents' names anywhere on the suitcase?"

"No. But yours was."

"There was a name tag?"

"No. Dr. Zimm gave you your name. He derived it from the title of the scientific paper. Dr. Zimm was the first to call you Max Einstein."

Leo went silent.

"Is that it? Is that everything Dr. Zimm knew?"

"Yes, Max. It is."

*It's not much,* Max thought.

*Ah, but it's a start,* said the kindly Einstein in her head. *Don't forget, I spent a good deal of time in Princeton, New Jersey, too!*

Could there be more clues to her past waiting to be discovered there?

# 19

The next morning, still frustrated that Leo didn't really know that much about her past (and realizing that Dr. Zimm had been lying to her all along when he promised to tell her "everything you ever wanted to know"), Max and the other seven members of the CMI team made their way to Rhodes House to hear Sir Gordon Richards speak about world hunger.

That's why Max had only a banana for breakfast.

After last night's world hunger banquet—and still thinking about that 70 percent of the world who have to get by every day on a single bowl of rice—she wasn't all that hungry. She even turned down the extra Kit Kat bar Siobhan had snagged out of the basement vending machine.

Charl and Isabl went with the CMI team to the lecture

hall. They had their sunglasses on and their pigtail ear-pieces in. They were running security. Ms. Kaplan stayed behind at the dorm to, as she put it, "refine our upcoming leadership exams." Yep. As long as Ms. Kaplan was around, there were going to be tests. Lots and lots of tests.

Max didn't think Professor Einstein would agree with Ms. Kaplan's techniques. "Teaching should be such that what is offered is perceived as a valuable gift," he once said, "and not as hard duty."

Ms. Kaplan was all about the hard duty.

Max thought Sir Gordon Richards's talk on the same stage where Albert Einstein spoke way back in 1931 was fascinating. She could understand why Ben wanted the Change Makers to hear what he had to say.

"Last night," said Sir Richards, "seven hundred and ninety-five million people went to sleep hungry."

"Yeah," muttered Keeto. "I was one of them."

"That's more people than the population of the United States and Europe combined. Not having enough food makes hunger, and, of course, malnutrition, the number one public health risk worldwide—far greater than AIDS, malaria, and tuberculosis combined."

"Ben certainly didn't choose an easy assignment for us this time," whispered Annika.

After painting a grim picture about the problem, Sir

Richards went on to outline a few possible solutions. Max took notes.

"We should produce less biofuel for our internal combustion engines and use food for, well, food. Here's a hard one for me: we need to stop our first-world meat feast. Forty percent of grain crops are currently going to feed cows, pigs, and fish instead of people. We must endeavor to support small farmers. Particularly, small farms owned and operated by women. And, finally, we must encourage economic growth. More trade and open markets will help the flow of food."

Sir Richards ended his lecture by declaring that the 193 member states of the United Nations had agreed to an amazingly big goal: ending poverty and hunger by the year 2030.

That wasn't too far away.

Max and her team, plus people all over the world, would definitely need to help the UN if it was ever going to achieve its goal.

After hearing Sir Richards speak, Max and her friends were stoked. They started batting around ideas as they strolled back to the dormitory.

"I like what he said about eliminating meat from our global diet," said Hana.

"Because you're a vegan," said Klaus. "You ever eat vegan sausage?"

"Yes," said Keeto. "It's not bad."

"Speak for yourself."

"More women farmers," said Siobhan. "Works for me."

"Did you know," said Annika, who liked to gather random facts to use in her logical arguments, "that if women farmers had the same access to resources as men, the number of hungry people in the world could be reduced by one hundred and fifty million?"

"Says who?" asked Klaus.

"The FAO."

"Who are they?"

"The Food and Agriculture Organization of the United Nations."

"What do you think, Max?" asked Tisa.

"That you're all right," she answered. "For a problem this large, we may need to try a little of everything!"

"We'll talk about it more when we land in America," said Charl.

"Whoa," said Keeto. "We're heading back to the United States?"

Isabl nodded. "Ben just texted us our new marching orders. We're to fly to America. He wants us to work with the Institute for Advanced Study at Princeton University in New Jersey."

"Hey, Max," said Klaus, "isn't that where your buddy Albert Einstein did a lot of his research?"

"Yes," said Max. "He was at the Institute for Advanced Study from 1933 until his death in 1955."

"Princeton will be amazing," said Toma.

"Pack your things, guys. Ben's private jet is standing by. We'll be flying to Princeton ASAP."

Max smiled.

Because, if what Leo told her was true, she wasn't just flying to Princeton.

She was flying home.

# 20

The eight members of the Change Makers team, plus Charl, Isabl, Ms. Kaplan, and Leo, would all be driving in one large van to Kidlington, a privately owned airport about six miles north of Oxford.

Some of the kids, like Klaus and Tisa, had several enormous suitcases. Ms. Kaplan had half a dozen. Max figured most of hers probably had test booklets stashed inside them.

"There's barely enough room inside the van for all twelve of us," said Charl. "We'll need to stow the bags and gear up top."

"I can be of assistance in that regard," said Leo. "I have industrial-strength hydraulic arms, capable of hoisting several hundred pounds." Then he giggled.

Once all the suitcases, duffel bags, and Leo's travel box

were bungee-corded to the roof, the van looked like a great white whale of a pack mule with too much cargo on its back.

Isabl studied the mountain of luggage perched on top of the van and sighed. "This is going to limit my ability to drive the way I like to drive."

Max grinned. She knew how Isabl liked to drive. Fast. And furiously.

Everyone piled into the van. Max, Klaus, and Leo took seats on the rear bench.

"Everybody in?" asked Charl, doing a quick head count. "Good. Let's roll."

Groaning under its heavy load, the van lurched away from the stately castle of a dormitory.

"I want to remind everyone about our competition for the best new ideas," said Ms. Kaplan once the trip to the airport was underway.

"Competition?" moaned Tisa. "Why can't we all just collaborate?"

"Because," said Ms. Kaplan, "competition fires up one's adrenaline and leads to more and better ideas. Think about your solution to world hunger on the flight. Whoever has the best idea will be the new team leader. The new *chosen one*." She looked at Max when she said that. "What? Did you somehow think your position was permanent?"

Max's face remained emotionless. She wouldn't rise to

Ms. Kaplan's bait. She didn't want to do anything that might jeopardize her chances of going to Princeton, the place where Dr. Einstein spent his final years. The place where Max might've been born!

"Warning," Leo suddenly chirped. "Threat level adjustment. Significant. Imminent."

"What?" said Klaus.

"I am picking up Corp communications," Leo said with a nervous giggle. "They have us, and I quote, in their sights. Triangulating the radio transmission, I suspect they might be currently located . . . right behind us."

"You're just now telling us this?" cried Klaus, tugging at his hair. "You're supposed to give us an early warning alert! This, Leo, is not early!"

Max whipped around.

Their groaning passenger van was being pursued by a sleek black SUV with a tinted windshield.

"It is Professor Von Hinkle," Leo reported. "He has a strike team. Seven members. Four male. Three female. All should be considered heavily armed and extremely dangerous. Suggest initiating evasive maneuvers."

"In this hulking box?" shouted Isabl. "Wish me luck!" She jammed her foot down on the gas pedal. The speedometer budged forward maybe one mile per hour. She yanked the steering wheel hard to the right, to swerve around a slow-moving truck. The van felt like it might tip over on its side.

"They're gaining on us!" shouted Toma, who never did all that well in tense situations. "We're all gonna die!"

"Correct," remarked Leo. "If conditions remain stable, I would put the probability of death or imminent capture at ninety percent."

"We're not gonna die or be captured," said Max, who'd been assessing the situation and coming up with a solution.

"Yes, we are!" whined Toma. "There's nothing we can do to escape."

"Yes, there is. Leo? Can you and your hydraulic arms pop out that window?"

"Of course," replied Leo. "However, since this is a rental vehicle, Charl and Isabl will be liable for any damage, such as a broken window."

"We'll pay!" shouted Charl from the front seat. "What's our play, Max?"

"The same as always," replied Max. "Physics! Pure and simple."

# 21

"Slow down, Isabl," said Max, calmly.

"Are you bonkers?" asked Siobhan.

"If we slow," said Leo, "the Corp vehicle will be on our bumper in approximately one minute."

"Slow down!" Max repeated. "I have an idea!"

Isabl eased off the accelerator.

"Leo? Punch out the window."

"Again, I must remind you of the liability issues associated—"

"Punch it out!" shouted Klaus.

Leo did.

Air whooshed through the hole, creating a swift shift in air pressure. Everything that wasn't strapped down inside the van was sucked through the empty window frame as if it were a vacuum cleaner.

"Okay, Leo," coached Max. "Now I need you to crawl out and use those hydraulic muscles of yours to unsnap the nearest bungee cord."

"If I do that—" Leo began.

"The outside force of the wind will cause the bodies at rest, in this case, the luggage, to no longer be at rest. All the stuff will go flying. Backward!" Max said triumphantly.

"Bombarding the bad guys behind us!" said Klaus. "Awesome!"

"But those are our suitcases," said Hana. "All my clothes, my..."

"My suitcase has all my memories in it," said Max. "And I'm willing to lose it if it means we all get to the airport alive."

"Do it, Leo!" said Charl. "Initiate the baggage bombardment."

Leo pivoted his torso and, powering up through his hips, stuck his head and arms out the empty window frame. "Standing by to release cords," he chirped, his words and giggles whipped away by the wind.

"Isabl?" said Max. "Reaccelerate. Let's give that wind even more velocity!"

Inertia, keeping
object in place.

Bodies at rest being acted
on by an outside force
i.e. wind.

Force = Mass x Acceleration

Accelerated suitcase, filled with the mass
of Ms. Kaplan's shoes, equals enough
force to shatter windshield.

"Roger that, Max!"

"Leo? Let it rip!"

One of Ms. Kaplan's suitcases slammed into the SUV's windshield.

"My shoes!" she screamed.

"Good," said Max. "They have a lot of mass, which means, after accelerating, they smashed into the SUV with a ton of force."

Other suitcases pummeled the car tailing the CMI van as Leo kept popping more bungee cords free. His travel box shattered into splinters when it slammed into the SUV. Max saw her prized, antique suitcase fly into the hulking black vehicle's shiny chrome grille. It must've hit the sweet spot because the hood popped open, blocking the driver's view.

The SUV swerved too hard to the right. It went up on two tires, flipped, and rolled over and over into a ditch, landing upside down.

If Max had to lose her beloved suitcase and her lifetime collection of Einstein memorabilia, this was a good way for it to go.

"They are still alive," reported Leo, sliding back into the van. "They are also very angry."

"You still picking up their radio transmissions?" asked Max.

"Affirmative. However, I am pleased to report, Professor Von Hinkle and his associates are the only Corp strike team currently operating in the United Kingdom. They had no backup or plan B. Therefore, I estimate we have at least a thirty-minute jump on them. Given current traffic conditions and congestion as reported by Google Maps, it will take at least that long for them to commandeer a new vehicle."

"Step on it!" shouted Keeto.

"No problem," said Isabl, as the van zoomed forward. "This soccer van moves a lot faster without all that extra baggage and wind drag up top."

"We know," said Toma, who seemed much calmer now that the Corp had been temporarily knocked out of the game. "It's physics!"

# 22

With no luggage, the team boarded Ben's private jet in record time.

They moved even faster after Leo reported the latest radio transmission intercept from the Corp strike team.

"Those members of the Corp strike team who are still mobile have, at gunpoint, hijacked a van. They will arrive at our location in approximately three minutes."

"We need to hustle, people," said Isabl. "Fasten those seat belts. Fast!"

"Wait," said Ms. Kaplan, as Charl closed the main cabin door.

"What's wrong?" said Charl.

"What about the van? Shouldn't we return it to the rental agency?"

"We have already alerted them of its location on the tarmac and apprised them of the damage done to the rear window. Ben will pay for it."

"But I left something in it," stammered Ms. Kaplan. "A bottle of Pravastatin. It's my heart medicine."

"When did you last take it?" asked Max.

"This morning!"

Max turned to the robot with the incredibly deep artificial intelligence. "Leo?"

"The Mayo Clinic recommends taking Pravastatin once a day, at the dosage level prescribed by your doctor."

"She'll live," Max said to Charl. "I'm pretty sure they have drugstores in New Jersey. We'll find you a refill, right after we land, Ms. Kaplan. Right now, we need to be in the air, flying away from England and Professor Von Hinkle."

Ms. Kaplan nodded and returned to her seat.

"Seat belts, please," said Leo, whom Klaus had quickly programmed to assume all the duties of a typical flight attendant.

Charl and Isabl sat up front in the cockpit. They were both licensed pilots but Ben's private jet didn't really need their assistance. The thing was fully autonomous and could fly itself, once you told it where you wanted to go.

"Trenton-Mercer Airport in New Jersey, please," Isabl said.

"Calculating route," said a soothing female voice from the control panel.

The engines started spinning. A few seconds later, the jet was gliding out to the runway.

"Um, could you ask this thing to scoot a little faster?" said Keeto. "The bad guys are on their way, remember?"

"We should be wheels up in two minutes," reported Charl.

"We are number one for Runway Five-Niner," purred the voice inside the console. "Flight attendants, kindly take your seats."

"Yes, ma'am," said Leo, strapping himself into a jump seat behind the bulkhead.

As the plane began to roll toward the runway, Max glanced out her window. A red minivan with a bunch of stuffed animals came screeching onto the tarmac and braked right where they had boarded. A huge man emerged and stared after them, but he was too far away for Max to see the expression on his face.

Seconds later, the sleek jet was airborne.

Max collapsed back into her seat. She'd wanted excitement, but that was a little too much all at once.

When they reached a comfortable cruising altitude, Leo came up the aisle to offer everyone an assortment of snacks and beverages.

"Snack?" he said, holding out a basket filled with chips, fruit, and cookie packets. "Beverage?" He was dragging a cart loaded down with soft drinks, cups, and ice.

"Is this really a good use of his incredible AI?" asked Keeto.

"Works for me," said Klaus, grabbing a fistful of peanut bags and a sack of sugary cookies.

"You realize," said Hana, "you now have more calories in your grubby paws than most humans are able to consume all day?"

"Hey, there wasn't any rice or dirty water on the cart," said Klaus. "Give me a break."

"We're supposed to be coming up with solutions to world hunger, Klaus," said Annika. "Not stuffing our faces."

"Well, I can't think on an empty stomach."

"You can't do anything on an empty stomach," snapped Keeto. "Because your stomach has never been empty."

"It was at that hunger banquet last night. For at least an hour. Longest hour of my life…"

The others laughed and joked and started tossing around ideas for combating world hunger. (One was to put Klaus on a diet so other people had a chance to eat.)

Max and Ms. Kaplan both remained surprisingly quiet, lost in their own thoughts.

Max had no idea what Ms. Kaplan was thinking about. Maybe her missing heart medicine. Maybe her lost shoes.

Meanwhile, Max was focused on one thing and one thing only.

And it wasn't world hunger.

It was her own, personal past at Princeton.

# 23

**The group arrived without incident (or luggage) at** Princeton.

First stop was the Princeton University Store where Ben's credit card bought everyone new clothes, most of which had tigers (the Princeton mascot), the Princeton shield, or just a simple capital "P." The clothes—mainly sweatshirts, sweatpants, and T-shirts—were black, orange, and various shades of gray. The University Store also sold underwear, socks, and sneakers.

"We're good to go," said Klaus, who loved his new Princeton hoodie.

Princeton University was nearly as impressive as Oxford. It was founded in 1746 and had what Max thought was a very interesting motto: *Dei Sub Numine Viget.*

Translated from Latin, that meant "Under God's Power She Flourishes."

*I flourished here,* said the imaginary Einstein in her head. *You should flourish even more. After all, you're a "she"!*

The campus was filled with stately stone buildings that had webs of ivy crawling up their walls. Many of them, like those at Oxford, reminded Max of churches.

Max knew that Dr. Einstein loved living in Princeton during his "banishment to paradise." He had moved to New Jersey to escape the rising threat of the Nazis in Germany. In the run-up to World War II, he wrote that he felt privileged to live in Princeton, which he likened to a calm island in a sea of conflict. "Into this small university town the chaotic voices of human strife barely penetrate. I am almost ashamed to be living in such a place while all the rest struggle and suffer."

Max hoped there would be time in her schedule to visit the Albert Einstein home at 112 Mercer Street.

"We will start working on our World Hunger Project with the Institute for Advanced Study first thing tomorrow morning," Ms. Kaplan announced.

Max was eager to visit the IAS, too. After all, Albert Einstein was one of its first professors.

"This evening, kindly check into your assigned rooms at Mathey College. Then, finish whatever shopping you need to do as a result of losing your luggage. You are also responsible for your own dinner, as well."

"Do we have to eat rice and dirty water again?" asked Keeto.

"No," said Ms. Kaplan. "The dining hall offers an extensive selection of first world foods—everything from braised beef brisket to cheese and onion mashed potatoes and coconut pudding cake."

"Um, are you trying to make us feel guilty about having food?" asked Tisa. "Because, if you are, it's totally working!"

Later, when Max went down to dinner, she saw Toma, the astrophysicist from China, sitting at a table all by himself.

"Mind if I join you?" she asked.

"Not at all."

Max sat down and started eating her pasta. Baked ziti with shrimp.

"So, are you as pumped as I am to be here?" said Toma. "I mean, this is Princeton! Einstein was here—doing all sorts of heavy thinking about wormholes, gravity, and time travel." Toma's eyes darted back and forth, as if he wanted to make sure nobody was listening to what he said next. "I've already made first contact with someone from the Einstein Time Travel Institute."

"Does that actually exist?"

Toma nodded.

"Cool. Where are they?"

"Right here in Princeton, Max! That's why I'm so excited. The ETTI was big back in the 1920s. They were doing all sorts of fascinating stuff. Now, most people kind of laugh at them. Well, him. There's only one guy keeping the ETTI alive. But, to me, time travel would be the maximum application of Einstein's theory of general relativity."

Max looked startled. Probably because Toma was using the same string of words that had been in the title of the scholarly article that, according to Leo, had been tucked into her suitcase along with that first photo of Einstein.

"You okay, Max?" asked Toma when he saw the look on her face.

"Yeah. Fine. It's just, you know, I'm interested in time travel, too."

Especially right here in Princeton.

If she could go back in time to the 1930s, could she actually meet her hero, Albert Einstein?

If she could go back a dozen years, could she meet herself?

Better yet, could she meet her parents?

"Toma?" she said. "Have you set up a meeting with your contact at the Einstein Time Travel Institute?"

He nodded. "Tonight. Ten p.m."

"Great," said Max. "I'm coming with you."

# 24

"When I'm older," Toma told Max between bites of his salad, "I'm going to Mars. We'll need astrophysicists up there."

"We?" said Max.

"China. Sun Laiyan, the person in charge of our National Space Administration, has China doing deep space exploration focusing on Mars. Our first spacecraft, without any crew on board, will go to Mars before 2033. Spaceships with crews will start landing there in 2040; maybe a little later. I'll be the perfect age for the first flight!"

Max grinned a little. She couldn't help thinking about how timidly Toma behaved in high-stress situations. She wondered how well he would do strapped down inside the tip of a rocket blasting off for Mars.

"You ever read science fiction?" Toma asked.

"Not much," said Max. "I prefer science fact."

"You should read fiction, too. It's what happens when facts get tumbled inside a writer's imagination. And you know what Einstein said..."

"Imagination is more important than knowledge."

Toma nodded. "Imagination is what got Professor Einstein thinking about warping time—just like in a science fiction book!"

Max, of course, knew that Einstein imagined that time could be warped in the presence of a major source of gravity—like, say, a black hole in outer space. A black hole is where gravity has become so strong that nothing around it can escape, not even light. The closer you are to a star or planet or black hole—anything with big-time gravity—the more time will warp.

Einstein's theory of General Relativity showed that time passed slower for objects near strong gravitational fields than for objects far away from them.

"If, Max, you could get close to a black hole," the Einstein in her head had once explained, "the passage of time, for you, would slow to a relative crawl. If you escaped and returned to Earth to tell your friends about your incredible adventure, they wouldn't be there because, even though you only thought you'd been gone for a few weeks, thousands of years would have passed on your home planet."

That meant time travel, at least into the future, was possible.

"Guess what, Max?" said Toma eagerly.

"What?"

"Darryl says they did it."

"Who's Darryl?"

"The guy trying to keep the Einstein Time Travel Institute going. He's a grad student. Everybody at Princeton thinks he's a fool. Anyway, Darryl told me that, way back in the 1920s, when Albert Einstein was visiting the campus, two very clever young scientists did the impossible. They took Einstein's theory of general relativity and made it work. They took the complex and made it simple. They made a time machine!"

# 25

Professor Von Hinkle arrived in Princeton a few hours after the CMI team.

He couldn't fly to New Jersey on the Corp's SST jet. None of the airports in the Garden State would allow his sonic boomer to land on their runways. Noise issues from their neighbors, undoubtedly. So, after the car crash (which put five members of his tactical team into an Oxford hospital) he had to scramble and arrange a new ride back to America.

A private jet owned by a Corp subsidiary company in England was at his disposal—after he confessed that, like Dr. Zimm, he had once again let Max Einstein slip away.

"I will apprehend her," he promised the board.

"You'd better," he was advised. "If you fail again, you

123

will be sharing an icy cold cabin in Greenland with Dr. Zacchaeus Zimm."

Tracking Max to America, Professor Von Hinkle decided it would be better if he traveled alone.

Moving with a group of thuggish mercenaries made him far too easy to spot. Max and her minimal security team could see the small army coming from a mile away. Communicating with his minions over radio headsets made tracing his movements even easier. After all, the Corp had designed the automaton Lenard with the ultimate in electronic eavesdropping capabilities. The robot was, undoubtedly, continuously monitoring all frequencies, running search algorithms that would identify any and all potential threats to its new mission.

Professor Von Hinkle, much like a machine with artificial intelligence, gathered this new data, learned from it, and adapted. He improvised.

He now knew he had a better chance of capturing Max Einstein and the traitorous bot Lenard on his own.

Of course, he wasn't completely alone. He still had his aluminum attaché case filled with the miniature drones. The ones with the nasty array of needles.

Von Hinkle, leaning on a cane, limped into Princeton's Peacock Inn. He had been slightly injured when the SUV flipped over on the way to Kidlington. Nothing too serious.

Just enough to slow him down and make him despise Max Einstein and Lenard even more.

They'd definitely pay for what they had done. Once the Corp had everything it wanted from Max and Lenard, the professor would extract his personal revenge.

Princeton's Peacock Inn, a renovated colonial-style mansion from the eighteenth century, was set on a tree-lined street. It was a lovely little hotel. Charming. Quaint, even.

But that's not why Professor Von Hinkle had chosen it for his base of operations.

Oh, no. He had selected it because it was a six-minute walk (seven with a cane) to the Princeton campus. The drones, with their heat-seeking guidance systems, could cover the same distance in sixty seconds.

His asset on the ground shadowing the CMI team kept feeding Professor Von Hinkle real-time updates. "Your best chance will come at night," the source informed him. "Max is prone to taking long walks after dark to contemplate her Einsteinian 'thought experiments.' Lenard will be sharing a room with Klaus, the blubbery boy from Poland. He will not offer you or your team any resistance. The boy is a coward."

Von Hinkle still hoped to snatch and grab both targets. But, if he were forced to make a choice, he would go for the girl and come back later for the bot.

He snapped open the attaché case and examined the twelve miniature drones, all of them sleeping peacefully in their charging slots. He connected a USB cable to a port built into the side of the case and plugged its other end into a wall outlet.

He then called the front desk and ordered room service. A simple turkey sandwich. With two pickles.

"We all need our batteries recharged and operating at one hundred percent of capacity," he whispered to the shiny metal orbs. "Because, very soon, one of you is going to make Max Einstein sleepy. Very, very sleepy."

# 26

A little after ten o'clock that night, when all their CMI teammates were fast asleep thanks to jet lag, Toma and Max met up under one of the streetlamps glowing in front of the residence hall.

Against the night sky, the building loomed behind them like a medieval castle.

"Should I go wake up Charl and Isabl?" asked Toma, looking around nervously.

"What for?" whispered Max.

"In case those guys who are always chasing after you decide to chase after you again tonight."

Max sighed. Toma was the most timid member of the CMI team. "You can relax. Leo puts the current Corp threat level at one percent."

"What? It's not at zero?"

"Leo doesn't believe in a zero percent threat. He says something could always go sideways. So he's hedging with that one percent. He's a computer. He doesn't like to be wrong."

"Well, if there is any kind of threat level at all, we should probably take a security detail..." said Toma.

"Charl and Isabl will just tell us to go back to bed. We're not in Princeton to explore Einstein's theories of time travel. This is an extracurricular activity. Now where is this guy Darryl?"

"At the Time Travel Lab."

"And where's that?" asked Max.

"Actually, it's just a study room inside the Firestone Library. He was able to borrow it from a friend in the Department of Comparative Literature. Darryl said he'd meet us there at ten-thirty. We're supposed to bring him a cup of coffee and a doughnut."

"Then we'd better hurry," said Max.

Max and Toma made their way across campus to the Firestone Library. They were able to grab a cup of coffee and a granola bar at a small café in the lobby.

The grad student named Darryl met them in a third-floor study room.

"This the kid named Einstein?" he asked.

"Yes," said Toma.

He handed Darryl the white sack from the lobby shop. Darryl pried open the flip lid on the coffee container and started slurping. Loudly.

"You bring me a doughnut?" he asked.

"They didn't have any," said Max, gesturing toward the bag. "So we got you a granola bar instead."

"Granola bar?" Darryl whined. "I seriously wish you kids could go back in time and get my order right. A granola bar is in no way an adequate substitute for a doughnut. Especially a glazed doughnut. The kind they make with yeast."

"Sorry," said Toma.

Max thought about lecturing Darryl about all the starving kids who'd love to have a granola bar or anything besides dirty water and rice but decided not to go there.

"Going back in time would be so cool," said Darryl, sucking down some more coffee. "But it's a billion times harder than going forward."

He went to a whiteboard mounted on one wall of the study room and started scribbling numbers, all of which Max completely understood.

"Every astronaut who ever went into space was a time traveler. Because of time dilation, they return to Earth very, very, very slightly younger than their twins who remained home, if, you know, they have a twin. But, if you want to go back in time to pick up a proper doughnut? That's almost impossible. I mean you *could* try to go faster than the speed of light, I guess, but I don't recommend that."

Max nodded. "Me neither. Einstein's equations say that an object moving at the speed of light would have its mass increase toward infinity while its length shrank down to zero."

"Exactly. And you can't pick up a doughnut when you're that massive but tiny."

"You could look for a wormhole," said Toma. "A tunnel through space-time."

"It's a longshot," said Darryl, slurping more coffee. "And you'd probably end up in the past in another part of the universe..."

"But Toma told me that the Einstein Time Travel Institute did build a time machine," said Max.

Darryl nodded. "Long, long time ago. Back in 1921. When Albert Einstein was visiting Princeton to give some lectures and pick up an honorary degree. Dude named Dean West called Einstein 'the new Columbus of science, voyaging through the strange seas of thought alone.' This was before Einstein moved here full time. Some people think it's just an urban legend. I think it's true. There was a time machine in the basement of the Tardis House!"

"Tardis House?" said Toma.

Max shrugged. She had no idea what Darryl was talking about, either.

"That's what I call it," said Darryl. "What? Don't you kids watch *Doctor Who*?"

"I'm afraid not," said Max. "Is it a TV show?"

"Uh, yeah. Only the best TV show ever. It's British. Been on since 1963. The Doctor is a Time Lord from the planet Gallifrey, who explores the universe in a time-traveling space ship called the TARDIS, which, on the outside, looks like a big blue police box. That's a telephone booth for cops to use. You guys know what a telephone booth is?"

"I've seen pictures of them," said Toma. "In history books."

Darryl gurgled down some more coffee. "Never mind. The Tardis House is over on Battle Road. It's all boarded up. Has been since The Accident."

"Accident?" gulped Toma.

"Yeah. From what I hear, Albert Einstein was lucky to get out of there alive."

# 27

Max and Toma followed Darryl as he led them off the Princeton campus and into the nearby streets.

"Einstein lived a few blocks over that way," said Darryl. "112 Mercer Street. These days, the houses are all pretty pricey on Battle Road. You'd think they would've torn down the Tardis House, but the feds won't let them, I guess. They keep it pretty secure. There are high-tech locks on the doors. Not exactly sure why. I mean, the place is a dump. Guess the powers that be don't want anybody sneaking inside and learning the truth."

"And what's that?" asked Max.

"That way back in 1921 two brilliant professors built a time machine in that house! Einstein said the young couple understood him and his theories better than he understood them himself. Anyway, this couple invited Albert Einstein over one night to show off their invention, which, by the way, took up the entire basement."

"They seriously built a time machine?" said Toma.

Darryl shrugged. "That's what everybody says. They were way ahead of their time. Problem was, whatever they cobbled together ate up too much electricity and power. Then it started feeding back, looping on top of itself. Made the temperature plunge. Ice formed on all the windows. The time machine collapsed in on itself and disappeared. So did something else."

"All their designs and drawings?" said Toma.

"Worse. Their daughter. A small child! The absent-minded professors had left their kid down in the basement. After the accident, she was just gone. Vanished. There was no way she could've survived that energy burst. Her mother and father, of course, were devastated. They left Princeton, disappeared, and never pursued their time-travel experiments again."

They arrived at 244 Battle Road.

It was a darkened, sagging house with sheets of plywood nailed over all the windows. The homes on either side were stately and impressive brick structures.

"That one there on the right?" said Darryl. "Number 246? It has some pretty cool history, too. A nest of intellectual property thieves used to operate out of it. Spies who stole all sorts of research from folks doing classified work on campus. When the feds raided the place, like twelve years ago, everybody and everything was gone. Nothing was left inside except a few sticks of furniture."

Max stepped forward into a pool of light. She looked up.

There was a smoky dome concealing a surveillance camera. It was attached to the streetlamp's post. Her image was being picked up. If the Corp was paying attention, they might be able to use their facial recognition software and pinpoint her location.

*I don't care,* Max thought. *I need to be here.*

There was something about 244 Battle Road that kept pulling her closer. It was a black hole exerting its time-warping gravitational field on her.

"You want to take a peek?" said Darryl. "There's a window around back where there's a busted-out knothole in the plywood."

"Then can we go inside?" asked Max.

"No way," said Darryl. "The alarm system is super sophisticated."

"We can't risk it," said Toma, sounding anxious again. "One peek and then we should go back to the dorm."

Max hurried around to the rear of the house. She found

the hole in the plywood covering one window and peered inside.

The house was dark. But as Max's eyes slowly adjusted, she could make out a few shapes and forms. One of those lumpy shapes turned into a dusty suitcase covered with cobwebs.

It was the very same style as the one Max had, until very recently, carried with her wherever she went.

She wanted to rip off the plywood and crawl through the window to take a closer look. But she saw the wire strips leading to magnetic contacts. Like Darryl said, the rickety old house had a highly sophisticated burglar alarm system.

Somebody wanted to keep people out.

Suddenly, a searchlight thumped on behind Max. She was standing in a circle of blindingly bright white light.

"Freeze!" somebody shouted.

They'd found her.

# 28

*The security camera!* thought Max.

Raising her arms over her head but not turning around, Max remembered what Leo had told her about Dr. Zimm. That he'd found Max crawling around in a basement. *"The basement was situated in a place called Princeton, New Jersey. Not far from the university where Dr. Zimm was doing intellectual espionage work for the Corp."*

According to Darryl, the house next door to the Tardis House had been a den of intellectual espionage agents. Was that where Dr. Zimm found Max and her suitcase? Could she have been the baby who crawled through the space-time fabric, altering her time (by decades) and her space (by maybe fifty feet)?

"Max?" cried a familiar voice. "Are you all right?"

It wasn't Professor Von Hinkle or a squad of Corp goons. It was Charl.

Whoever was manning the floodlight switched it off. Max turned around and saw that the backyard of the Tardis House was extremely crowded with shadowy figures.

"We told you not to leave the dorm," said Isabl, who'd made the trip with her partner.

So had about half a dozen campus security officers and a pair of officers from the Princeton Police Department.

"Darryl McMasters," said one of the police officers, shaking his head. "I thought we told you to leave this house alone."

"I was just walking down the street, man," Darryl lied. "There's no law against that, is there?"

The police officer's partner rolled her eyes. "I will be so glad when they tear this place down next week."

"What?" said Darryl. "They're tearing it down? The Tardis House?"

"Who are the Tardises?" asked the cop.

"Never mind," said Darryl. "But you can't tear the house down. Albert Einstein visited here once."

"You want us to arrest you so you can tell it to the judge?"

"No," said Darryl. "Hey, Toma."

"Yeah?"

"Lose my number." Darryl stuffed his hands into his pockets and shuffled up the sidewalk.

"Thank you for your assistance, officers," Charl said to the campus and Princeton police. "We'll take it from here."

"These two," asked one of the campus police, "are they part of the genius squad? The kids who are supposed to save the world?"

"That's right," said Isabl.

The officer shook her head. "Poor world. We don't stand a chance."

Max and Toma climbed into the CMI van.

"I'm sorry," Max said.

"Me, too," added Toma. "But the house really is historically significant."

*Especially to me,* thought Max. *Maybe.*

"Why's it so special?" asked Charl as Isabl piloted the van back toward the Princeton campus.

"Back in 1921, they did Einsteinian time-travel experiments there," said Toma, excitedly. "They took the theory of general relativity and pushed it to the max."

"It's dangerous for you two to be roaming the streets by yourselves," said Isabl, looking at them through the rearview mirror. "You know that."

"We had Darryl," said Toma. "And he's a grad student."

Max stared out the window and watched the campus

buildings roll by. Most looked like they'd been there since forever. She was seeing the same Princeton that Albert Einstein probably saw all those years ago.

What she couldn't see, however, was the miniature drone following the van.

# 29

**Almost.**

Professor Von Hinkle sat in his cozy room at Princeton's Peacock Inn, monitoring the drone video feed on his laptop computer.

He'd almost had her.

His advanced facial recognition software had picked up Max Einstein's image on the streetlamp surveillance camera. She was far enough away from her security detail for an efficient strike. Three drones from his squadron of twelve was all it would've taken. Two to lethally inject the Chinese boy Toma and the bumbling grad student Darryl. One to administer a sedative to Max.

But the CMI security team had swooped in before the remotely controlled drones could attack. And, to make matters worse, they were accompanied by campus and township police. Apparently, they had facial recognition software, too.

If Professor Von Hinkle had gone ahead with the hit, it would have been a wasted shot.

No, Von Hinkle would wait for his next opportunity, which hopefully would come at a location without so many antagonistic law enforcement agencies close at hand.

His undercover asset would make certain of it.

If they didn't (and soon), Von Hinkle might send a lethal injection drone after them, too.

After all, he had a dozen of them.

# 30

The next morning, Max joined the rest of the CMI team for breakfast.

"Where'd you sneak off to last night?" Siobhan asked.

"Just another stop on my tour of old Einstein haunts," said Max. "A place where they did some interesting work related to his theory of general relativity."

That was all Siobhan got. No honest confession that Max might've visited the house where she used to live, way back in 1921, until, in a freak accident, she time-traveled forward into the future, which turned out to be everybody else's present.

It sounded so ridiculous, Max didn't even believe it herself.

Yes, it probably would've been good to talk about her

thoughts and feelings with a friend like Siobhan. But Max Einstein still didn't know how to confide her deepest feelings with anybody, even her best friends, without making herself vulnerable. She'd lived by herself for too long, she figured. She was too street smart and cautious from her years as a homeless orphan. The first twelve years of her life had taught Max that she really couldn't trust anyone—except, maybe, the imaginary Einstein in her head.

After breakfast, the team members were told to report to a study room in Mathey College.

The desks had been outfitted with cardboard privacy screens.

"What are those for?" asked Klaus.

"So you won't be tempted to copy answers from your neighbor's answer sheet," replied Ms. Kaplan. "Kindly find your seats. The initial examination will commence in three minutes."

"What?" said Keeto. "Is a doctor coming to check us out? Make sure we're up to date on our shots?"

The kids laughed. Ms. Kaplan did not.

"This will be a test of your knowledge about world hunger. Its root causes and current statistics. It will cover all the material I asked you to familiarize yourself with."

Max looked to Tisa.

Neither one of them loved taking tests.

"Most teachers waste their time by asking questions that are intended to discover what a pupil does not know, whereas the true art of questioning is to discover what the pupil does know or is capable of knowing."

-Albert Einstein

Neither one of them had studied for this one.

Max took her place behind one of the cardboard privacy screens. She stared at the exam booklet and the answer sheet filled with rows and columns of circles for her to fill in with a number-two soft lead pencil.

"You may now break the seal on your exam booklet," Ms. Kaplan announced.

Max used the sharply pointed pencil tip to slice open the circular sticker keeping it shut.

The booklet was filled with questions about world hunger facts with multiple-choice answers.

Max glanced at the first one.

1. What percentage of food is wasted and never consumed after being grown, processed, and transported in the United States?
   ○ 10%
   ○ 20%
   ○ 30%
   ○ 40%

Max assumed the answer was 40 percent. She'd seen how wasteful Americans could be with their food during her years as something of a dumpster diver. There were always big bags of doughnuts or bagels being tossed out behind New York City's bakeries every night. She used to gather up the bags and take them back to the stables where she lived to give her other homeless friends a feast.

But, instead of answering the question (or any of the ninety-nine others), she started looking for patterns in the answer sheet filled with circles. She ended up connecting the dots to draw the Big Dipper, the Little Dipper, and several other constellations.

Her mind was floating through space, visualizing one of the basic concepts of general relativity: that stars and planets warp the fabric of space-time, making time travel possible. *Making her journey forward from 1921 possible?*

An hour later, when Ms. Kaplan called time, Max turned in her decorated answer sheet and received another circle.

A big, round zero.

She'd flunked the exam.

Her days as the CMI's "Chosen One" might be dwindling down to a big round "zero," too.

# 31

After the exam, each member of the team was expected to present their best idea for eliminating world hunger.

Ms. Kaplan and a panel of judges from Princeton's Institute for Advanced Study, where Albert Einstein had been one of the first professors, would listen to the ideas and help determine the best of the best.

Max knew that the founding director of Princeton's IAS had believed that if it steered clear of "the chase for the useful," then "the minds of its scholars will be liberated." In other words, the Institute wanted to set thinkers free and not focus on results. They let scholars take advantage of surprises, hoping that "someday an unexpected discovery" might open up new worlds and new solutions.

The IAS was big on blue-sky thinking. Brainstorming with no limits and no expectation of practical applications for their discoveries. This was pure Einstein. So much of Max's hero's genius came from these thought experiments. He loved thinking for the sake of thinking. Max did, too.

It's probably why she wasn't great at regurgitating facts for a fill-in-the-circles exam.

Tisa, the biochemist from Kenya, went first. She stood before the panel of judges, seated in the front row of a large lecture hall, and advocated supporting small farmers. Especially in third-world countries.

"A combination of money and education in low-tech concepts such as better rice planting and irrigation, coupled with better seeds and fertilizer, could spark a green revolution back home in Africa!" she told the judges.

"We need to roll out more biotech, big time," said Klaus when it was his turn. "I'm talking genetic modification, people. Yes, I know it gets a bad rap in the developed world, but think about it in real-world applications: we could gene-splice plants so they could withstand droughts and floods. We could play with the genetic code of pigs and chickens to engineer their stomachs and intestines so they'd eat food humans don't need and maybe make them poop less, too, which, hello, would help us with clean water problems!"

The judges didn't look too happy with Klaus's idea. In fact, several looked like they might lose their lunches.

Siobhan talked about easier access to credit. "The big banks need to help the little farmers." Annika discussed the logic of urban farming, since nearly 25 percent of under-nourished people live in cities. Toma had some wild, bluer-than-blue-sky ideas about colonizing Mars and setting up "remote agricultural stations" on Jupiter's moons. Keeto suggested creating an app directly linking farmers with consumers.

Hana, the vegan botanist from Japan, went second to last and talked about her vision for sustainable food. "We must farm and grow food in a way that can be done forever," she said. "No more dependence on cheap energy powering huge farm machinery. No more petrochemical-based fertilizers and pesticides. Food should be sold locally through farmers' markets and local shops. We need to go organic. It's kinder and gentler to the land and animals we all need to survive." Then she started sounding like she was running for office. "The answer to world hunger, my friends, lies not in handouts of free food but in build-ing local systems of production and distribution that can withstand shocks such as war, drought, and disease—ensuring that nutritious, sustainable produce is always available."

Several judges' heads were nodding when Hana finished. A couple even clapped.

Then it was Max's turn.

"Whatever we do," she said, "we should start small. Prove that it works. And only then ask others to scale it up for us. There's no way a group as tiny as ours can solve a global problem as huge as world hunger without the help of many, many others."

"What?" scoffed Klaus. "Start small? Come on, Max. Go big or stay home. We're the Change Makers! We don't do anything in a small way."

The young geniuses were asked to leave the lecture hall while the judges and Ms. Kaplan deliberated.

The CMI team didn't have to wait long for the decision.

Hana's sustainable food idea was quickly deemed the best. Ms. Kaplan declared her the new Chosen One.

"And Ben concurs with my decision," she added. "Max? We look forward to your help in implementing our new leader's vision."

In other words, Max Einstein had just been officially demoted.

# 32

**"We should field-test Hana's sustainable farming idea** ASAP," said Ben over a speakerphone set up in one of Mathey College's common rooms.

The entire CMI team, including Leo, was huddled around the device.

"The sooner the better, sir," said Hana, sounding super confident in her new role as the team leader.

"Um, you can call me, Ben, Hana. 'Sir' is what people used to call my father. I'm just Ben. And since we'll be working more closely together now...first names are fine with me...if, you know, they're fine with you."

Max was wondering if Ben and Hana would start going out for private Chosen One lunches, the way Max and Ben used to.

Was Max jealous? No. Of course not. Okay, maybe a little.

"We should move our base of operations to West Virginia," suggested Ms. Kaplan. "It ranks as one of the hungriest states in America. Fourteen-point-nine percent of households in West Virginia suffer from food insecurity."

"Why not New Mexico?" asked Max. "It's the number one state for hunger issues. Seventeen-point-nine percent of the population is dealing with not having enough food."

Sometimes, Max remembered random facts like that. Usually when she didn't have to do it for a test.

"Then there's Oklahoma, Arkansas, Louisiana, Mississippi, and Alabama," she continued. "All of them are worse off than West Virginia."

"This is not your call, Ms. Einstein," said Ms. Kaplan dismissively. "Hana is in charge and she asked that I pick the location for our first field test."

Max looked down at the speakerphone. Ben didn't say a word. Yep. Her days as the Chosen One were definitely over.

"Besides, West Virginia is much closer to Princeton than any of the states mentioned by Ms. Einstein," Ms. Kaplan continued. "We can start implementing Hana's ideas almost immediately."

"I, uh, agree," said Ben. "West Virginia it is. I'll, you know, make some phone calls."

"I'm one step ahead of you, Benjamin," said Ms. Kaplan. She pulled a stack of papers and folders out of her briefcase. "I've done some preliminary research. There are some local organizations already doing sustainable agriculture work in Central Appalachia. They've set up shop not far from Shepherdstown, West Virginia. A green business lender in the area received a major grant from the Department of Agriculture to enhance farm-to-fork delivery. In other words, there are existing groups and infrastructure we can work with."

"Cool," said Ben. "You're in charge, Ms. Kaplan. Well, you and Hana. I've got to run. Some kind of meeting. Keep me posted. Send me a text or something. Thanks. Bye."

Ben clicked off.

"West Virginia?" moaned Klaus. "Farming? I'm not sure I want to be a farmer. And Leo here isn't built for heavy labor outdoors."

"What Klaus says is true," said the automaton. "Mud and manure might seriously impair my delicate circuitry."

"Mine, too," cracked Keeto.

"We will keep Leo out of the fields," said Ms. Kaplan. "He can assist with logistics."

"Thank you, Ms. Kaplan," chirped the robot.

"Great," said Klaus. "I'll assist Leo with his assisting."

"No, Klaus," said Hana. "I want you in the field with the rest of us."

"And by 'field,' you literally mean like a cornfield, right?"

"Actually," said Hana, "until I can convince the locals to go vegan with me, we'll probably be working in fields where they grow hay to feed livestock."

Annika nodded. "Hay is currently West Virginia's number one crop. Interestingly, ninety-five percent of the farms in the state are family owned. That's the highest percentage in the US."

"Let's hope these families won't mind working with us," said Tisa.

"Are you kidding?" said Keeto. "They're gonna love us. They might even want to adopt us all! Even Leo!"

"That would be sweet," said Leo. "However, I have already found my forever home. With the CMI."

"Awwww," said Klaus. "Isn't he cute? I programmed him to say that." He rubbed the robot's shiny plastic hair.

Everyone cracked up, except Max.

"We will ship out first thing tomorrow morning," announced Ms. Kaplan. "Seven a.m. sharp."

As the others shuffled out of the room, Max remained behind.

She was doing another thought experiment.

This one was thinking about how she couldn't leave Princeton until she visited the Tardis House at least one more time.

# 33

Max needed to be prepared before she set out for 244 Battle Road again.

First stop was Tisa's room.

"So," Max asked her friend, "have you been able to put your portable chem lab back together after our luggage incident in Oxford?"

"A little bit," said Tisa. "One of the chemistry professors on loan to the Institute for Advanced Study helped me out. She even gave me a handy metal carrying case for my brand new chemistry set." Tisa placed the box filled with rattling jars and bottles on a table. "How are you doing putting your Einstein memorabilia collection back together?"

"Not as good as you. But that's okay. All that stuff was sacrificed for a good cause: us staying alive."

"Totally. So, what do you need, Max?"

"Have you got any acetic acid?"

Tisa popped open the clasps on her chemistry kit. "Yeah. Here it is. Also known as methane carboxylic acid." She pulled out a small jar filled with liquid. "What do you need it for?" She looked around to make sure no one was eavesdropping. "Are you having an ear fungus issue?" she whispered.

"Maybe," said Max.

"Well, be careful with it. The stuff stinks. Acetic acid is what gives vinegar its nasty odor."

"Thanks."

"So, you excited about heading to West Virginia tomorrow?"

Max nodded. "Definitely. I'm sure Hana will do a great job setting up the project."

"I hope so," said Tisa. "We're all kind of used to having you in charge, Max."

"Hana's got this one," she assured her friend. "Don't worry. It'll be another CMI triumph!"

"People still talk about us back home," said Tisa. "How we turned on the juice and brought electricity and light to places where they'd only known darkness. You were a great leader, Max."

"Thanks, Tisa. I couldn't have done much without your help."

Acetic acid in hand, Max set up the second part of her three-step plan. She used the CMI credit card Ben had given her (back when she was the team leader) to order a major pizza delivery from Jules Thin Crust on Witherspoon Street in Princeton. They had vegan and vegetarian options. Thirty minutes later, twenty-five steaming pies were delivered to a common room of Mathey College, courtesy of Ben. The aroma was strong enough to draw everybody out of their rooms, including several dozen college kids who weren't on the CMI team. The crowd mobbing the open pizza boxes was so huge, nobody noticed that Max wasn't there.

While everyone was distracted by the pizza drop, Max snuck out a fire exit and made her way to the nearest drugstore where she needed to buy two empty spray bottles and some household ammonia. *While you're there,* urged a small voice in her head, *pick up a water bottle and matches. Be prepared.*

So Max did.

Outside on the sidewalk, most of the ammonia went into one spray bottle. Once that bottle was tightly sealed and all the scent of ammonia had evaporated from the air,

Max carefully poured the very pungent acetic acid into the other sprayer.

Next, she broke off the heads of about twenty matches, dumped them in the bottom of her brand-new twenty-ounce water bottle, poured in about two ounces of ammonia, screwed the bottle's lid back on tight, and swirled the contents around.

In a few days, that mixture of sulfur and ammonia would become a stink bomb. Did Max need a stink bomb? Maybe not that night. But she knew she might soon.

She stuffed all the bottles into the baggy pockets of her floppy trench coat. The two spray triggers hung out as if she had just strapped on a pair of six-shooters from a cowboy movie.

Ready for action, she headed back to the Tardis House.

Crouching low, she crept along a hedge until, doing some elementary trigonometry in her head, she computed the angle of sight for a 360-degree surveillance camera inside a dome attached to a light pole at a height of twenty-five feet.

She knew precisely where she could step before the camera's motion detector would start detecting her motions.

Max wrapped a bandana around her nose and mouth because she was about to create some toxic fumes.

Aiming both of her spray bottles up at the motion-detecting camera, she pulled the triggers. The twin streams of liquids intersected. The acetic acid and ammonia mixed together to form a warming smokescreen in what Tisa (and every other chemist) would call an exothermic reaction. In other words, combining the two chemicals generated heat.

The motion sensor that triggered the security camera would be looking for changes in temperature. The heat created by Max's stinky ammonia-and-acetic-acid fog would increase the temperature of the air around the camera to 98.6 degrees and beyond.

Once it did, Max would be able to pass underneath undetected. There would be no noticeable shift in temperature.

She gave her chemical reaction a minute or two, watching the cloud of smoke billow up around the camera.

Then she strolled past the lamppost and onto the lawn of 244 Battle Road. The police wouldn't know anybody was anywhere near the place.

Because their high-tech, motion-activated security camera hadn't detected any motion.

# 34

Max scurried around the house to the back door and placed her two spray bottles on the stoop.

Like Darryl had told her, whoever was in charge of the boarded-up Tardis House had secured the back door with a high-tech keypad lock. That meant they cared about what was inside and its history.

At least they would care until it was bulldozed down.

But maybe the people who knew what actually happened inside 244 Battle Road were eager to see it torn down. To bury whatever had happened in the basement all those years ago.

Max knew she couldn't crawl through a window because they were wired to a burglar alarm system. She'd have to go through the door. And, if she could figure out the combination for the keypad, no one could accuse her of breaking and entering. She'd just be "entering."

She looked around to see what she could use to help her crack the lock's code.

Antique paint curled off the house's weather-beaten clapboard siding. She peeled away a pile of dried paint swirls and ground those flakes in her palm until they became a fine, gritty powder. Next, she placed her hand at the same level as the numbered keypad. Finally, she blew across the finely crushed powder while simultaneously lowering her hand, making certain to cover the entire keypad with a thin layer of paint dust.

When it all settled, Max noted which number on the keypad had the highest concentration of gray powder. Then she looked for the second most, the third most, and the fourth.

Max knew that when a finger touches a surface, it leaves behind an oily residue. That oily residue would act like glue. Each touch after the first will leave slightly less oily "glue" behind. So, to find the first number in the combination, all she had to do was look for the key with the most oil on it and, therefore, the most paint powder. She then followed the dust trail, in descending order of thickness, until she tapped in the correct four-digit code.

The lock popped open.

Max pushed open the door.

Her heart was racing as she fiddled with the flashlight app on the phone every member of the CMI team had been given as part of their field gear.

Yes, she was entering a house that Albert Einstein had visited. That was thrilling. Just like being backstage at the Royal Albert Hall.

*But this might also be the house where I lived when I was a baby,* she thought.

Or maybe she was just deluding herself. Maybe Max just wanted a more permanent connection to her idol, and the Tardis House legend gave her one. Maybe she was just a regular orphan that somebody had abandoned in a wicker basket on the front porch of the spy house next door, and Dr. Zimm made up the story about finding her in the basement.

Max swung her flashlight around the room. Its beam landed on that cobweb-covered suitcase—the one that looked like a slightly larger version of her old Einstein memorabilia case. Both pieces of luggage seemed to come from the same matching set. They were the same color. Had the same vintage look. The same padded leather handle.

Max swiped the thick coat of dust off the suitcase and pried open its brass clasps. Did this suitcase have a faded photograph of Albert Einstein tucked inside it like hers did? The smell of stale air that'd been sealed up for decades walloped her nostrils as she raised the lid.

There was no picture of Dr. Einstein. There was nothing.

She blindly ran her hand through a cloth pocket with a puckered elastic hem.

There was something inside the pouch. It felt like a photograph.

Max pulled it out.

It was a black-and-white portrait of an infant. A girl with a mop of curly hair tied back in a bow. Someone had scribbled the name "Dorothy" in the lower right-hand corner. Was that the photographer's name? The baby's?

Was that Max's real name?

Because the girl in the picture looked like a miniature version of the twelve-year-old Max, especially the wild mop of tangled curls. Was Dorothy's hair red, too? The black-and-white photograph didn't reveal the answer.

Max slipped the photograph back into the cloth pouch and closed up the suitcase.

"Guess I have a new place to store my Einstein stuff," she told herself. She'd definitely be taking the suitcase back to the dorm.

But first, she had to explore the basement.

Is this the baby picture I never had?

"If you want to make your children brilliant, tell
them fairy tales. If you want to make them
more brilliant, tell them more fairy tales."
                                            —Albert Einstein
Is this just a fairy tale I'm telling myself?

# 35

Max made her way down creaking wooden stairs that sagged with every step.

Her flashlight app could barely pierce the darkness as she descended. The house had no functional electric lighting. The narrow basement windows up near its ceiling were boarded over so tightly, no moonlight seeped in.

Max reached the concrete floor and shone her flashlight around the room.

The center of the floor was charred black—as if a rocket ship had used it as a launch pad. Looking up, she could see a tangle of ancient singed cables dangling from the ceiling, their cloth insulation frayed.

Something had been ripped out of this room. Something big and complicated.

*A wormhole generator?* But how could such a device even be possible, especially back in 1921?

Because the two young scientists who lived in this house were geniuses, just like Max and her friends. They, according to Einstein, understood his theories better than he understood them himself.

Max moved to the far wall. There was a blackboard that had been scrubbed clean. There was also a row of clunky, gunmetal gray filing cabinets. Max squeaked open a drawer.

Empty.

Someone had, probably a long time ago, come down here and scrubbed away every trace of what had happened in this basement. Hopefully, they took notes and photographs. Maybe they even saved the young geniuses' writings in a secret storage facility somewhere. Maybe the government had everything and would be happy to see the old house torn down—because they'd built their own time machine based on what was built here.

But all that was just wild speculation.

Max could see that there was nothing for her in the Tardis House except Darryl's stories and an old suitcase with a baby portrait tucked inside.

She climbed back up the staircase, thankful that none of the rotting treads collapsed as she climbed them. She grabbed hold of the dusty old suitcase on the first floor and carried it to the back door.

When she stepped outside, she froze.

Twelve hovering silver balls with fluttering humming-bird wings—resembling high-tech versions of the Golden Snitch from Harry Potter's Quidditch games—were arrayed in a pyramid formation directly in front of her.

The one in the lead actually started talking to her.

"This is Professor Viktor Von Hinkle," the drone droned through a miniature speaker. "Resistance is futile, Max. Stand where you are."

Max disobeyed the floating bot's commands. She immediately leaped back into the house and slammed the door shut.

She thought about using her phone. Calling the police. Calling Charl and Isabl.

But she'd already broken the rules and sneaked out of the dorm once. Charl and Isabl weren't big on repeat offenders, especially if you did the thing they already told you not to do.

The metal drone banged against the door. Hard.

"Work with us," the talking drone continued, its voice muffled by the wooden barrier. "We understand you have been demoted. That you are no longer the CMI's so-called Chosen One."

*What?* Max thought. *How could the Corp know that?* It just happened a few hours earlier.

"Work with us. With our unlimited resources, you and Lenard could revolutionize quantum computing as the world knows it."

Max ignored Von Hinkle's argument. She wondered how the Corp knew where she was.

The answer hit her in a flash: her phone had a GPS chip in it. That meant she could be tracked, if somebody knew her phone number. But only the CMI team had that information. Was there a CMI spy working undercover for the Corp again?

It seemed the only logical answer. *How else could the hovering drones have found her?*

She'd disabled the streetlamp security camera. She'd left the dorm without anybody knowing she'd snuck out.

*Hana,* she thought! She wanted to be the Chosen One so badly, she'd do anything to eliminate Max as a threat. Klaus had done something similar on an earlier project when he wanted to be the one in charge.

*It has to be Hana.*

Max knew she should worry about who turned her in later. After she survived whatever attack the squadron of Corp drones had in store for her. Could she outrun them?

Doubtful.

Unless...

She pulled the photograph of Dorothy out of the antique suitcase and stuffed it down into the inner pocket of her trench coat.

It was all she'd be able to take with her from the Tardis House. She'd be leaving the suitcase behind. There was no way for her to carry it.

Because she'd need two hands to handle the drones.

# 36

"It is time for you to forget this CMI foolishness and work for the Corp, Max!" said the lead drone outside the door. "Stay where you are. We are on our way to pick you up. If you tell us how to find Lenard, you will be handsomely rewarded."

*Yeah, right,* thought Max. *They'll make me watch while they dismantle the poor bot.*

This was her cue to leave.

She hunched down low, like a sprinter in the starting blocks. She dangled her arms down to the floor and flexed her fingers.

She had one shot at this.

One shot.

She took a deep breath. Raised her right arm. She

170

wrapped her hand around the doorknob and slowly twisted it to the right.

"Let us in while you wait for your pickup," purred Von Hinkle's voice from the drone. "We'll help you pass the time more comfortably."

Max waited a beat.

Then she yanked the door open, just as the lead drone shot forward to bang against it again.

Since the door was open, instead of slamming into wood, the dumb drone zipped into the darkened room. At the same instant, Max zipped out to the stoop in her hunched-over stance, her hands perfectly positioned to grab the two spray bottles she'd left there earlier.

She started running.

The cluster of drones remained locked in their hover positions. They didn't move.

*They must be taking orders from the lead guy,* Max thought. Good. That would make her job easier.

She raced across the lawn and dashed down to the street.

"Pursue her!" she heard a tinny voice say. "We need to administer the tranquilizer."

*Oh, no, you do not!* thought Max as, arms pumping, trench coat flapping, she ran up the street toward the Princeton campus.

The drones were speedy. She could hear their metallic

wings buzzing and clacking behind her. She dodged right and they stayed on her. She juked left, and so did they.

They were tracking her.

Suddenly, a lone drone flew in front of her, spun around, and nose-dived straight at her.

A needle was sticking out of the orb like a shiny little dagger.

Max whipped up both spray bottles and shot another intersecting-stream blast at her attacker. The exothermic reaction's toxic cloud threw off the drone's heat-seeking guidance system. Max sidestepped to the right again. The blinded drone's needle jabbed itself into the asphalt, missing her sneaker by an inch.

Max started running again.

Now she was on campus, not far from Mathey College.

The remaining unrelenting drones hovered in a cluster behind her.

"Surrender, Max," cried the lead drone. "We don't want to hurt you."

*Oh, yes, you do,* thought Max. *That's all you Corp goons know how to do. Hurt people.*

She whipped around. Studied the eleven silver balls lined up in a flying wedge, making it super easy to spot the lead drone.

She pulled up both spray bottles and aimed them at her primary tormentor.

"So long, Professor Von Hinkle," she shouted right before she gave the shimmering orb a double shot of ammonia and acetic acid.

The heat-generating smoke screen messed with the weapon's internal guidance system. That meant it also messed with the signals the queen bee was sending out to the ten worker drones still flying in its fleet.

Before long, the drones started wildly whirling and twirling through the air. A few slammed into each other, exploding. One snagged a power line and sent up a shower of electrical sparks. Drones dropped like tin bricks out of the sky. One dinged the hood of a car and set off its very annoying alarm. Another smashed through a stained glass window. Alarm bells started ringing. Max started running again.

She didn't want to be out on the street when the campus police showed up to examine the accident scene. Hopefully, they'd chalk up the drone wreckage to a brainy fraternity prank gone bad.

Max slipped into the lobby of Mathey College.

"Awesome pizza party, huh?" said Klaus, coming out of the common room with a paper plate. "This is my seventh slice!"

"Yeah," said Max. "I had three."

"No way. You had at least four or five. I saw you loading up your plate."

Max shrugged. "Busted."

"I just wish Ben had sent more with sausage," said Klaus. "Who wants vegetables on their pizza? Have a good night, Max."

"Good night, Klaus."

Max smiled.

Apparently her diversionary tactic had worked just the way she hoped it would.

Everybody was having so much fun gobbling down pizza, they'd assumed Max was there, too.

# 37

That night, Max had trouble falling asleep.

And not because Siobhan was snoring in the lower bunk (she was).

She just had too much on her mind.

Should she tell Charl and Isabl about her encounter with the Corp's drones? If she did, she'd have to admit that she did exactly what they told her not to do. Besides, the group was leaving Princeton first thing in the morning, heading to West Virginia. Max would stick close to Charl and Isabl in the morning. The Corp wouldn't dare strike again while she was protected. *Would they?*

*But how did the Corp know where to find me?* she wondered again.

At first she'd thought Hana might've alerted them to

her whereabouts in an attempt to eliminate any lingering threat she might pose to Hana's new role as the Chosen One. It's hard to be the new queen if the old one is still hanging around in the palace.

But that was probably something she made up because she'd been demoted. After being told she was the most brilliant of the brilliant, now she was being told she wasn't good enough.

Max had never sought out the title or position. But she had to admit, it felt good being selected for an honor like leading a team of genius kids. Now that had been taken away from her.

By Hana.

By Ms. Kaplan.

By Ben.

That demotion from Ben hurt the most. It would hurt even more if he started inviting Hana out to private lunches.

So making Hana a suspect, a spy for the Corp, made Max feel better. The only problem was, it didn't make sense. How would Hana even know how to reach out to Professor Von Hinkle or anybody else at the shadowy organization? Klaus had only done it accidentally with a phone he'd given Max that he didn't realize was actually a sophisticated tracking device.

No, the Corp probably discovered that she was in

Princeton the way they always discovered stuff: using highly sophisticated facial recognition software scanning the thousands of security cameras she hadn't noticed on her journey to Princeton.

*Maybe I should wear a disguise all the time like we did in London,* she thought.

And then there was all the stuff from the Tardis House for her to think about. The legend of the young couple. Their lost child. The photograph of baby Dorothy. The suitcase that looked so much like hers.

How it kind of matched up with what Leo had told her about Dr. Zimm. Had her whole life been nothing more than the result of a freak accident that happened way back in 1921?

"Focus on the task at hand, Max," said the gentle Einstein in her head.

"But what is that task? Finding out who I really am?"

"You don't need to worry about that, Max. You already know who you are."

"Um, no, I don't."

"Ah, but you should. You, my dear one, are a very gifted and talented young human being who can do much good in this world."

"But what if I time-traveled here from 1921?"

"Would it matter?"

"People like us, who believe in physics, know that the distinction between past, present, and future is only a stubbornly persistent illusion."
– Albert Einstein

"Uh, yes."

"Time is relative. The distinction between the past, present, and future is only a stubbornly persistent illusion.

"All any of us really have is today," the grandfatherly voice continued. "And today, your friends need your help solving this problem of world hunger."

"Actually," thought Max, "we're not leaving Princeton until tomorrow."

"Which will be today when it comes."

"True."

"Try to remember, Max: it doesn't really matter where you came from. It only matters where you are going and what you will do once you get there. Only a life lived for others is a life worthwhile."

"Okay," said Max, with a sigh. "I'll stop obsessing about the Tardis House. I'll focus on the hunger problem. I'll help Hana and the rest of the team."

And that was exactly what she intended to do.

But the next morning, at breakfast, where she was seated at a long table with Siobhan, she met Dr. Shannon McKenna from Princeton's Institute for Advanced Study, who paused to say hello as she made her way past Max's table. Dr. McKenna certainly looked like a professor. She was wearing a long white lab coat and had old-fashioned, carefully coiffed hair that was whiter than snow on rice.

"Toma and Darryl tell me you are extremely interested in the history of the house on Battle Road," she said to Max, handing her a business card. "If you ever come back to Princeton, please contact me. I know more about the 'Tardis House' than anybody still alive."

# 38

**Of course Max wanted to hear more.**

"How do you know so much?" she asked.

"Let's just say I'm older than just about everybody else at the Institute."

"B-b-but..."

Dr. McKenna smiled kindly, waved with the banana that seemed to be all she'd be eating for breakfast, and walked away.

Max wanted to chase after Dr. McKenna but Siobhan placed a gentle hand on her shoulder so she couldn't stand up from the table.

"Finish your gruel," said Siobhan, nodding toward Max's bowl of oatmeal. "Blimey. Did a rabbit poop in your bowl?"

Dilemma: a situation in which a difficult choice must be made between two or more alternatives, especially undesirable ones.

A) She carries a banana and hidden knowledge about the time travelers' house.

B) They carry hope for a starving world.

Go with A, disappoint B.

Go with B, lose knowledge available from A.

Max couldn't help but laugh.

"Those are raisins," she explained.

"Ah, yes. What happens to grapes when they drop to the ground, shrivel up, and die."

"I want to find out what Dr. McKenna knows about the Tardis House," Max whispered to her friend.

"And Ben wants us on a bus to West Virginia. Will what you learn from the white-haired wonder woman help wipe out global hunger, Max?"

Max shook her head. "No."

"Well, as a wise man once said, 'Only a life lived for others is a life worthwhile.'"

"You're quoting Albert Einstein."

"Am I now?" joked Siobhan. "And all this time I just thought it was something you scribbled inside the lid of that mangy suitcase you used to drag everywhere. Stay focused, Max. This team still needs you."

Max grinned and nodded. Siobhan, of course, had no way of knowing it but she was also quoting the Einstein inside Max's head. He'd urged Max to stay focused on the task at hand, too.

So, while Max spooned oatmeal and raisins into her mouth, she started thinking: *Is there a simple solution to this problem?*

Where is the simple scheme for ending world hunger?

Could the simple ever solve the complex?

*Yes! That's what Albert Einstein did all the time. He reduced complex problems to their—*

"You ready to roll?" Siobhan was gently shaking Max out of her trance.

"Hmmm?"

"They're loading up the van. We need to go, Max."

"And where exactly are we going?" she asked dreamily, as if she were half awake and half asleep.

Siobhan rolled her eyes. "West Virginia, Max. Focus, girl. Focus!"

Right.

Max really needed to start doing that.

# 39

Isabl was letting the automaton Leo drive the hulking black van, which had four rows to accommodate all eleven passengers.

"This is better than an autonomous automobile," remarked Klaus. "We have a chauffeur bot!"

"Woo-hoo!" shouted all the other kids.

Max had to admit: it was pretty cool having a robot behind the wheel. There was no need for a separate GPS device. The GPS that, of course, wouldn't work without Einstein's theory of relativity, was already inside Leo's brain.

"Thank you for this opportunity to be a true team player," said Leo. "I project arrival in the Shepherdstown, West Virginia, vicinity in approximately three hours and forty-five minutes. I, of course, will be happy to stop along the way should a majority of the passengers need to use the facilities. I myself will have no such need."

"Indeed," said Toma. "However, we should keep your charger plugged into the USB port so you don't fall asleep at the wheel."

"Never fear, Toma. I am fully charged. I have also pre-selected some instructional audio books to make the two hundred and twenty-three miles fly by."

"Yo, Klaus," said Keeto. "Did you give Leo a mute button? Because no way am I listening to four hours of boring textbooks."

"No need for audio entertainment, Leo," Klaus instructed the robot. "Just drive."

"Your wish is my command, Klaus," said Leo.

"Yeah," said Klaus, puffing up his chest. "That's a new response I gave him for whenever his voice recognition software picks up a command from me."

"Is there a Society for the Prevention of Cruelty to Robots?" wondered Annika. "If so, we are definitely turning you in, Klaus."

"Children?" said Ms. Kaplan, who was sitting up front in the passenger seat. "I suggest you use this transportation time wisely. Study your briefing books."

"Or grab a nap," mumbled Charl, closing his eyes and

leaning back and snuggling down into his seat in the second row.

"Wake me up if you need me, Leo," said Isabl, closing her eyes, too.

"I don't anticipate requiring assistance," Leo chirped. "I will simply obey all posted speed limits and traffic advisories."

Isabl grinned and shook her head. "How boring."

Max flipped through the three-ring binder that Hana and Ms. Kaplan had put together with all sorts of multicolored tabs for things like Project Goals and Objectives and something called Deliverables. Not to mention a timeline and a series of graphs and flow charts.

When Max was the team leader, she never planned out her CMI projects with this much precision and detail. She never organized everything in a binder. She just had brainstorms and figured out how to turn her big ideas into practical reality, one step at a time. It usually involved a lot of scribbling in notebooks or scratching a stubby chunk of chalk on a blackboard—or any other surface that was handy.

Max's style left room for improvisation. For changing things on the fly as a situation altered or conditions threw you a curveball.

Hana's technique was definitely more buttoned up. But what if the world didn't go along with her flow chart? What about surprises and unexpected discoveries? What about unanticipated disasters? They'd probably need to rewrite this action plan at least once or twice before they reached its goals.

Forget looking for a rest stop. Hana and Ms. Kaplan might need Leo and his internal GPS to find them an office supply store. Some place to buy more color-coded tabs for their silly binders!

# 40

As the van rolled through northern Maryland, Leo pulled off the interstate, cruised down an exit ramp, and made an announcement.

"We have now reached the halfway point of our journey," he said. And then he giggled. (Klaus just couldn't seem to erase that quirk from deep within Leo's circuit boards.) "We will stop here for a restroom and refreshment break. While you are inside, I will drive over to the gas pumps and refill our fuel tank."

"You guys hop out," said Isabl. "I'll ride over to the pumps with Leo. Don't want anybody to have a heart attack when they see a robot behind the wheel."

"They better get used to it," said Klaus, hauling himself out of the third row of seats. "Leo represents the future, the

189

tidal wave of autonomous automobiles that will soon be flooding these freeways, and there's no stopping it!"

"Unless," said Toma, "one could travel back in time and stop the development of the first robot."

"Actually," said the super logical Annika, "if you want to stop scientific advancement, you'd have to go back further than that."

"True," added Siobhan. "You'd have to go back and stop the caveman who invented the wheel. Maybe bop him on the head with a club."

"But what about the caveperson who invented the club?" said Tisa. "If you want to stop the arc of scientific development, you'll have to stop him or her, too. And the guy who made the fish hook…"

"And the first person to eat lobster," cracked Klaus. "He must've been very, very hungry!"

Max loved hanging out with the CMI crew. They could have a fun debate about anything.

She and Siobhan finally piled out of the van after all the others.

"Pick up a couple gallons of diesel fuel," said Charl. "We might need it for a generator when we're in the field."

"Will do," said Isabl.

Max spent some time in the rest stop's small snack shop,

where they sold all sorts of chips, candy bars, soft drinks, and plastic-wrapped baked goods. A guy in green coveralls was pulling prepackaged Honey Buns off a rack and putting them into a big bin.

"Excuse me," Max said politely. "What's happening with all that food?"

"I need to take it off the shelf," the man told her. He held up a package, turned it over, and showed Max a date printed on the plastic. "See? Today's its expiration date. We need to get rid of the stale stuff, load in some fresh items."

"And where will the expired food go?"

The man shrugged. "The garbage, I guess. Maybe a landfill."

"Would anything bad happen if someone ate, say, that expired Honey Bun you just pulled off the rack?"

"Not really. Packaged food like this can actually stay safe for a pretty long time after the sell-by or use-by dates. If, you know, it's handled and stored properly."

"Thank you, sir."

"You want a Honey Bun?" said the man, gesturing to a pile of them in his bin. "It's free. I'm gonna toss it anyway."

"Thanks," said Max, taking the wrapped-and-sealed swirl of fried dough drenched in a shiny white glaze.

She couldn't wait to taste it.

Not because she loved fried dough soaked with sugary sauce.

But because she was actually starting to have an inkling of an idea about how to fight world hunger.

# 41

Professor Von Hinkle limped over to the Princeton campus carrying his empty attaché case.

It was early afternoon. He had wanted to inspect the drone crash site sooner but needed to wait until the campus police and other local authorities had done their investigation. It took them all night and into the next day.

"Nerd Prank Gone Bad" became the official reaction to the incident, which did damage to several campus buildings and multiple vehicles parked in the street. Maintenance workers were sweeping up the last metallic shards of what had been Dr. Von Hinkle's flying fleet of armed drones. Two workers used a long pole to knock down a lone drone stuck in a tree. It clattered to the pavement and shattered.

The workers tossed its shiny shards into a black plastic trash bag.

The foam slots in Von Hinkle's weapons case would remain empty. His army of flying bots had been destroyed when, somehow, their infrared guidance system went haywire.

The angry professor would have to find some other way to subdue Max Einstein and force her to work for the Corp. He had not reported his latest failure to the board of directors, as it was just a minor, temporary setback.

Because he knew precisely where Max Einstein was.

At a rest stop in Maryland. Eating a glazed Honey Bun.

Yes, his intelligence was that good.

And what was even better?

His undercover asset would soon deliver Max to West Virginia.

Which just happened to be the Corp's backyard.

# 42

When the CMI team reached West Virginia, their first stop was a church.

"Um, why exactly are we stopping here, Leo?" asked Keeto from the third row.

"Because your new team leader, Hana, instructed me to do so," the boy-bot replied.

"I thought this would be an instructional stop for all of us," said Hana. "Twice a week, this church operates a food pantry out of its basement. This will be a chance for us to see the true face of American hunger. Tisa? Can you please give us the stats?"

"Hang on," said Tisa, flipping through her binder. "There's no tab for stats..."

"They are filed under Background," Hana told her.

"That's the blue one?"

"Right. B for Background. B for Blue."

"Got it," said Tisa. "Okay. In the aftermath of what has been labeled 'The Great Recession of 2008,' families today do not visit food pantries only for emergencies. Food pantries have become an important part of many households' long-term strategies to supplement monthly food budget shortfalls. And get this—more than half of this food pantry's clients are people with jobs."

"And they can't afford food?" said Toma.

"That's right," said Hana. "These days, families with minimum wage jobs have to choose. Food, medicine, transportation, or housing."

"But food pantries aren't a long-term solution to the hunger problem," said Klaus.

"No," said Hana. "They're not."

"The building is secure," said Charl, coming back to the van. He and Isabl had done a quick sweep of the church, to make certain no hostiles from the Corp were hiding under the pews or up in the bell tower.

Everybody trooped inside and took the stairs down to the basement.

Max surveyed the scene.

A multitude of people—some elderly, some clutching

196

children's hands, some wearing work uniforms—were lined up in a hallway that led to a half door where a volunteer put assorted food items like apples, cereal, and rice into an empty banana box. Every family received one carton of food. All the cartons were the same.

Max found her sketchbook and started doodling.

*This could be done better,* she thought. *The same food could be delivered with more dignity.*

"You guys?" she said when the CMI team regrouped in the Sunday school room down the hall from where the food was being handed out. "What if they set this up differently? What if, instead of giving everybody a box of the same food, they gave out, I don't know—coupons. Something like, three proteins, two starches, four fruits and vegetables. Then, the church could put all the food on shelves, like they do in a supermarket. They could use this room. I'm guessing it's always empty during the week."

"True," said Keeto. "Because Sunday school usually only happens on Sundays."

Max kept going. She was pumped. "The food pantry's clients could roll grocery carts through the aisles and check out with their coupons. It'd be a lot more dignified than shuffling up to take whatever someone else decided to give you in an old banana box.

"If they did that," said Max, "the whole experience

Old way: everybody gets the same pre-packaged box of food.

New way: clients choose. Everybody takes what their family really needs.

Food + Choice = Nutrition + Dignity.

would feel more like a trip to a grocery store, and less like a handout."

"Great idea, Max," said Siobhan.

"Fantastic," said Tisa.

Hana looked a little hurt. And Ms. Kaplan was giving Max the stink eye.

"I think you are forgetting something, Max," she said sternly.

"You're right. Milk and dairy. They'll need a cooler case for cheese and eggs and stuff."

Ms. Kaplan shook her head.

"No, Maxine. What you are forgetting is this: You have been demoted. You are not in charge of this operation!"

# 43

"Come on, Max," said Siobhan. "Let's go help them pack up those banana boxes."

"Good idea," said Tisa. "It'll help take your mind off... other things."

Max nodded and did her best not to let anybody see how much Ms. Kaplan's words stung her. She wasn't trying to be in charge. She had just been having an idea, a brainstorm, and was eager to share it. Siobhan and Tisa were true friends. They knew what Max was feeling even without her having to tell them.

"In two hours, we are due at the farm where we'll be doing our fieldwork," Hana announced, after checking the timetable in her Master Plan binder. "It's a thirty-minute drive so we can spend another ninety minutes here."

"I suggest you all use that time studying the green tab in your binders," said Ms. Kaplan. "Sustainable Farming 101. It will give you an overview of what we hope to accomplish during our time with the Carleigh family, who own the farm where we'll be doing fieldwork."

"If it's all right with you, Hana," said Tisa, flashing her brilliant smile, "Max, Siobhan, and I are going to work with the food pantry folks and do some in-depth end-user research. It'll give us, as you said, a better understanding of the true face of American hunger."

"Sounds like a plan," said Hana. "I look forward to hearing your full report."

"And we look forward to giving it," said Siobhan.

Max couldn't help but grin. Siobhan and Tisa were laying it on thick. Giving Hana exactly what she wanted to hear.

The three friends left the Sunday school room.

"Suck-ups," Max whispered when she was certain Hana and Ms. Kaplan couldn't hear her.

"Hey, it worked, didn't it?" said Siobhan. "We got you away from Ms. Kaplan."

The three went into a storage room where a volunteer showed them how to pack each box.

"Every client gets the same thing," explained the volunteer. "That way, there's no squabbling. Thanks for helping out. I need to go work the window."

The volunteer left. And as they packed the correct number of cans and boxes and sacks into each cardboard carton, the three friends started to chat.

"So why does Ms. Kaplan hate me so much?" Max wondered out loud.

"I have a theory," said Tisa. "You remind her of who she used to be."

"Huh?"

"I bet, when she was our age, the young Tari Kaplan was full of idealism. She probably had all sorts of ideas about how to save the world."

"And that would make her hate me...because?"

"Because," said Siobhan, "Ms. Kaplan didn't just grow up. She grew cynical. She probably thinks she was an eejit for ever thinking she could change the world."

"So she takes it out on you, Max," said Tisa.

"Interesting," said Max. "So when, exactly, did you two get your degrees in psychology?"

Her friends laughed.

"We're just bloomin' brilliant," joked Siobhan.

When all the crates were loaded with the appropriate allotment of food, Max and her friends walked up the line of people waiting to pick up their emergency groceries. They introduced themselves. Listened to the hungry people's stories. Shared some hugs and even a few laughs.

Max met a girl named Sam who reminded her of a younger version of herself.

"We both have boys' names," Sam said. "Makes us tougher."

"I guess so," Max told her. "You know, I used to be homeless."

"Really?" said Sam, who looked to be eight or nine. "That's so sad. We still have a home."

"We just come here to take a little pressure off our food budget," explained Sam's mom.

"My mom and dad are smart," said Sam. "They take really good care of me."

"And that," said Max, with a smile and a breaking heart, "makes you a very lucky girl."

Because Max had never had a mom and dad.

She never had a home of her own, either. Except, maybe, when she was a baby. Maybe then she had a house.

On Battle Road in Princeton, New Jersey.

Far from where she was standing now.

# 44

"Given current traffic conditions, we should arrive at the Carleigh family farm in approximately twenty-seven minutes," announced Leo from behind the wheel of the CMI team's van.

"Any signs of a skateboard park, Leo?" asked Keeto.

"Negative."

Keeto sank down in his seat. As a city kid from Oakland, he really wasn't enjoying the whole "back to the farm" aspect of this CMI assignment.

Max had a window seat in the rear row. When Leo stopped at a traffic light, Max's gaze drifted over to a grocery store where an employee was pushing a cart loaded with fruits, vegetables, and meat packages to a dumpster.

A coworker was already there, heaving bulging plastic bags into the big metal box.

"You think they're throwing away food?" said Toma, who had the window seat in front of Max and was watching the same scene.

"Sure looks like it," said Max.

"What a waste."

Farther down the road, Max saw a restaurant worker repeating the same ritual: dragging a pair of fifty-gallon rubber barrels stuffed with food out to a dumpster where a busboy was already tipping trays full of leftovers.

"Question," said the ever-logical Annika, who'd also been watching the restaurant workers throwing away the heaps of food. "How can there be a food crisis in America when so much food is being tossed away by Americans?"

"Pick up the pace if you can, Leo," said Ms. Kaplan. "We don't want to be late for our first meeting with our farming family. We're expected at the Carleigh home in ten minutes."

"You want me to drive?" asked Isabl, the speed demon.

"No, thank you," said Leo. "I will increase my speed to the maximum allowable by law and road conditions."

"Do it now!" snapped Ms. Kaplan.

Logic problem: how can there not be enough food when so much food is thrown away every day?

The solution to world hunger? Food!

"Throwing away food is like stealing from the tables of those who are poor and hungry."
    - Pope Francis

The scenery outside the van's windows turned into a blur of greens and browns. They were in farm country.

Max couldn't stop thinking about all that food she'd seen being thrown away.

She filed the images away in the mental binder she was secretly putting together. She was working on a big idea.

One she wouldn't share with the CMI team.

Because, as Ms. Kaplan had already reminded Max (at least twice), Max wasn't in charge. She'd been demoted.

And even for someone who never used to care about being in charge of anything (except her own life), that really, really hurt.

# 45

Professor Von Hinkle piloted his hulking black SUV down a rutted dirt road.

The car bounced every time it hit a pothole. Von Hinkle was so tall, his head hit the ceiling at every bump in the road. The SUV's churning tires spat up gravel and rocks, dinging and denting the vehicle's undercarriage. Von Hinkle didn't care. It was a rental.

He had to take the back way to the Carleigh family farm in rural West Virginia—where Max Einstein was due to arrive at three o'clock—because he couldn't risk his approach being observed by the CMI security team.

His undercover asset had informed Von Hinkle that the duo known as Charl and Isabl were extremely well trained by Israeli security forces. They were also extremely well armed.

And so he took the back roads only farmers took.

A little after three, he would finally apprehend Max Einstein and the AI robot code-named Lenard and haul them both up to the Corp's secret mountain hideaway in West Virginia.

In a series of coded messages with his contact, Professor Von Hinkle had mapped out his snatch-and-grab attack in minute detail.

The tactical team guarding the child prodigies would be lured away by a diversionary tactic to be determined once the asset assessed real-time conditions on the ground. Once the security personnel were removed from the scene, Max Einstein would be sent back to the group's van (for her own safety), where Lenard would be seated behind the wheel. Professor Von Hinkle would be able to acquire both targets in one fell swoop.

Luckily, West Virginia was a state that made it easy to purchase firearms. Early that day, Von Hinkle had purchased several of them.

He may not have his fleet of drones, but he had a shotgun. Max Einstein would be his in under an hour if everything went according to plan.

Which it had to.

Because Professor Von Hinkle was the mastermind behind it.

# 46

The CMI van arrived at the Carleigh family farm a little before three in the afternoon.

"Everybody out of the van," said Ms. Kaplan. "Except you, Leo. Your appearance may shock Mr. and Mrs. Carleigh and their children."

"Yeah," said Keeto, "that plastic face and hair still freak me out a little."

"Power down," said Hana, flicking the switch on Leo's back.

"Pow-er-ring dooooooown," slurred Leo as his head slumped forward and bobbled against the steering wheel.

"Take it easy, Hana," said Klaus, climbing out the sliding side door. "You could've permanently dented his forehead."

"Sorry," said Hana.

"Perhaps you should delegate some of your responsibilities," said Annika. "Let Klaus handle Leo's operation."

Hana ignored her and nodded toward the farmhouse porch where the Carleigh family—a mom, a dad, two sons, and a daughter—stood waiting expectantly.

"Good afternoon," said Hana, leading the group to the porch. Ms. Kaplan walked beside her. Charl and Isabl brought up the rear, scanning the vast fields for intruders and potential hazards. They patted their vests in that way they sometimes did to make sure their weapons were where they thought they were.

"We're from the Change Makers Institute," Hana said to the farm family.

"And we're here to help," added Keeto.

"Thank you for dropping by," said the farmer. "I'm Kurt Carleigh. This is my wife, Hannah. Our sons, Tyler and Quentin. Our daughter, Grace."

Hana quickly introduced the members of her team. She saved Max for last.

"Max Einstein?" said Mrs. Carleigh. "Any relation to Albert Einstein?"

"Hardly," said Ms. Kaplan with a backward snort.

Hana pressed on. "We wanted to talk to you about sustainable farming."

Mrs. and Mrs. Carleigh nodded.

"We studied that in agriculture school at West Virginia University," said Mr. Carleigh.

"That's where we met," said Mrs. Carleigh, smiling and giving her husband a hug. Their kids giggled, which made Max smile.

Hana just nodded and continued with her well-rehearsed speech.

"Then, as you might recall from your college studies, the goal of sustainable agriculture is to meet society's food needs in the present without compromising the ability of future generations, such as your children, to meet their own needs."

The famers nodded, maybe hoping Hana would finish her lecture and give them some practical tips on what they could do better. She didn't. She plowed ahead. She talked about turning manure into fertilizer and using rainwater for irrigation.

The farmers were starting to fidget. Mr. Carleigh checked his watch. His daughter started swinging her doll. The two boys looked like they wanted to run inside and play video games.

"Wait a second," said Ms. Kaplan. "Charl? Isabl? Did you see that?"

"What?" said Charl.

"Movement in the barn."

"Could've been one of our pigs," said Mr. Carleigh.

"We need to be sure," said Ms. Kaplan. "Go check it out."

Charl and Isabl nodded.

"You folks should probably go inside," Isabl told the Carleighs.

"Why?" asked Mrs. Carleigh, moving in front of her children. "What's wrong?"

"Probably nothing. But, to be safe..."

"Come on, everybody."

The farm family hurried into their house.

Charl and Isabl moved to the barn.

"Max?" said Ms. Kaplan. "Head back to the van."

"Excuse me?" said Max.

"Head back to the van! Now!"

"Why?" demanded Siobhan.

"If someone is in that barn," said Ms. Kaplan, "chances are it's the Corp, here to try to kidnap Max. *Again*."

"Then she shouldn't be alone," said Tisa.

"Everybody gather around Max," said Annika. "Form a circle."

"If they want Max," said Klaus, puffing out his chest, "they have to go through me."

"And me!" said Keeto.

213

"Uh, yeah," said Toma, trying his best to be brave.

All the teammates, including Hana, circled around Max and eyeballed the horizon, scanning it for intruders.

"No!" said Ms. Kaplan. "Max is supposed to go to the van. Leo can protect her."

"Um, Leo's shut off," said Klaus. "Remember?"

Ms. Kaplan tried to push the friends apart.

"Back off, you bloody cailleach!" shouted Siobhan. "Leave Max be."

That's when a black SUV suddenly appeared on a distant hilltop. It was maybe a half mile away.

It gunned its engine and barreled through the swaying hayfield.

Straight toward them.

# 47

**Max pushed against her friends, who strained to hold** her back. "Let me go! I'm pretty sure they want me alive."

She located the weakest link in the human fence penning her in and shoved Toma aside. She ran away from the farmhouse. The instant she did, the SUV changed its trajectory.

Max ran another twenty yards. She wanted her friends and the farm family out of harm's way.

The SUV was maybe fifty yards away now.

Max slammed on the brakes and dug in her heels. Then she propped her hands on her hips, thrust out her chest, and defiantly stared down the charging black bull of an SUV.

*Unstoppable force,* she thought, *meet immovable object.*

And, of course, while she stood there, solid as a rock,

215

some part of her brain whizzed off to analyze that statement. If an unstoppable force exists, then no object is immovable; if an object is immovable, then no force is unstoppable.

The driver of the SUV must've been having the same logic debate.

Because they also slammed on their brakes, churned up chunky clods of sod, plowed a pair of fresh furrows, and skidded sideways. When the vehicle stopped swerving, its driver's-side door ended up just ten feet away from where Max was standing.

The door swung open.

Out stepped a giant of a man with a huge, pineapple head. He was wearing a long black coat and toting a shotgun. Max recognized him immediately from her London briefing with Ben.

It was Professor Von Hinkle. The new goon from the Corp. Dr. Zimm's nefarious replacement. He stood at least seven feet tall in his chunky military boots, which were sinking into the muck of the hayfield.

"Get in the vehicle, girl," Von Hinkle grunted. *"Now."*

Max glanced over to the barn where Ms. Kaplan had sent Charl and Isabl. She saw a reflected glint up in the open hayloft. In her head, she quickly did some basic trigonometry and stepped two paces to her right.

"I said, get in the vehicle!" snarled Von Hinkle, limping two feet to his left, matching her move.

Max took another two steps. Once again, Von Hinkle mirrored her action. He was now eight feet away from his hulking SUV, putting him precisely where Max wanted him to complete a certain isosceles triangle.

"I suppose you want Leo, I mean, Lenard, too?" Max asked calmly.

"Yes," sneered Von Hinkle. "I will go to the van and acquire him, too."

Max nodded. Of course Von Hinkle knew that Leo was sitting, slumped over in sleep mode, behind the wheel of the van. Because Max also knew who told Leo to stay there. The same person who'd just ordered Max to go wait in the van.

The same person who'd been telling the Corp where they could find Max and her friends all along.

# 48

"I suppose you'll want to grab Ms. Kaplan while you're at it, too," said Max in a voice loud enough for all her friends to hear it. "How long has she been working for the Corp? I bet it's longer than she's been working for the CMI."

Von Hinkle glared at Max. Then he turned toward the group clustered in front of the farmhouse.

"Tari!" he shouted. "It's time to initiate your extraction package. Move!"

"She's on their side?" shouted Klaus.

"Blimey!" exclaimed Siobhan.

"Stop her, you guys!" said Keeto. "Don't let her get away."

Max saw her friends, including Hana, holding on to Ms. Kaplan. Restraining her from escaping.

"Let her go!" shouted Von Hinkle, raising his shotgun and aiming it at Max's chest. "Or little Miss Einstein dies."

Max's friends immediately released their grip on Ms. Kaplan's arms.

"Foolish idealists," she spat at them. "You're wasting your time helping others when you should be helping yourselves!"

"Like you did?" said Tisa.

"Yes, ignorant child. Like I did!" She slogged across the field toward the SUV as fast as she could.

"Oh, by the way, I'm sorry," Max said to Von Hinkle.

"For what?" He limped forward. "Causing that car wreck in England? Giving me this limp?"

"Yeah. That. And what's about to happen to your other leg."

"My other leg?"

"The one with the red dot. Right there. On your thigh? See it?"

There was a tiny laser point glowing on the right leg flap of Von Hinkle's long black coat. It would be point A at the end of the hypotenuse of a right triangle where Isabl, up in the hayloft with her sniper rifle, would be point B.

$$\sum_{i=1}^{M} (y_i - g_i)^2 = \sum_{i=1}^{M} \left( y_i - \sum_{j=0}^{P} w_j \times x_{ij} \right)^2$$

$$J(\theta) = \sum_{i=1}^{n} \| B_i \|$$

Yes, cowboys need math and physics, too!

The red dot exploded with a spray of blood.

An ATV came racing out of the barn.

Von Hinkle collapsed, as if somebody had knocked his legs out from under him, which, come to think of it, Isabl had done with a perfectly placed shot to the meaty portion of his thigh.

Meanwhile, Charl was on the four-wheeled all-terrain vehicle twirling—Max couldn't believe it—a *lasso* he must've found in the barn.

Charl tossed the lasso at Ms. Kaplan like a champion rodeo roper. He snagged her in the loop and yanked back hard to take out the slack and tighten the lasso wrapped around Ms. Kaplan's legs.

With a shriek, she face-planted in the mud.

Max's friends raced over and surrounded her, which left Charl free to zip over to where Professor Von Hinkle lay sprawled on the ground.

"We're going to need the first aid kit, Max," said Charl, climbing off the ATV so he could kick away the shotgun Von Hinkle was straining to reach. Charl pulled out a pistol and pointed it down at the muddy giant while patting him down to find any other guns. "We're also going to need for you to not move another inch, Professor."

"I'll go grab the first aid stuff," said Max.

She ran to the van and pulled open the driver's-side door.

The first aid kit was under Leo's seat. But his frozen legs were locked in place. Max felt along his back. Found the power switch and gave it a good bop.

Leo whirred to animatronic life and sat up straight. "Hello. Greetings. Welcome. Did I miss anything?"

# 49

"Why'd we come to West Virginia in the first place?" moaned Toma.

"It was Ms. Kaplan's idea," said Hana. "In truth, I thought New Mexico would be a better fit. The food crisis stats were better."

"And by better," said Annika, "you mean worse?"

"Precisely."

"So this whole excursion was a bloomin' setup?" said Siobhan. "A spy trick by Ms. Tari Kaplan to put Max right where she and the Corp wanted her."

"But why would the Corp, or anybody, want her in West Virginia?" said Keeto. He quickly turned to their hosts, the Carleigh family, who had set up a long table covered in a red-checked tablecloth to serve the CMI kids a farm fresh feast. "No offense. Your farm is lovely. But does West Virginia even have a city?"

"Several," said one of the sons, who didn't seem too happy to be sharing the bowls of mashed potatoes and platters of fried chicken with a group of city slicker snobs, even if they were supposed to be geniuses.

"The choice wasn't Ms. Kaplan's alone," said Max. "Ben was involved."

"He's the one who contacted us," said Mr. Carleigh. "Young feller named Ben Abercrombie."

"He's our benefactor," explained Hana who, technically, was still in charge of the team, even if one of the judges who had appointed her had just been revealed to be a mole. "Ben is our primary financial backer."

Ben had also made a few calls when Charl and Isabl told him what had happened. How Tari Kaplan had betrayed him and the CMI.

"How could she do something like that?" Ben had mused. "Why would she betray us and all we're trying to do?"

"Probably because you're an idealistic kid!" Siobhan had hollered in the background during Ben's video chat with the security team. "Ms. Kaplan, on the other hand, is a bitter old prune."

Charl and Isabl had handcuffed Ms. Kaplan and

Professor Von Hinkle with zip ties. Eventually, the state police and the FBI came to haul the two mud-caked Corp employees away. Neither one of them spoke a word after they were apprehended. Max figured that's what the Corp taught them in spy school.

"So why'd that gentleman in the black coat want you so badly, Miss Einstein?" asked Mrs. Carleigh.

"Because she's special," said Klaus sarcastically.

"Yeah," added Keeto. "For some reason, this evil multinational conglomerate called the Corp wants Max to work for them."

"They think they need her to build a quantum computer," said Toma. "So they can rule the world."

"Having Max on our team has proven to be quite a burden," sniffed Hana.

"Lay off her, Hana," snapped Siobhan.

"Yeah," added Tisa.

"I'm sorry. I don't mean to be rude. I'm just citing facts. Max is a target. And when she travels or works with us, we all become targets."

"I hate to admit it," remarked Annika, "but there is a great deal of logic to what Hana is saying. If Max wasn't on our team, we could focus more on our mission..."

Siobhan's temper was rising. "Are you forgetting the time Max saved your butt over in Israel, Annika?"

"No. I'm remembering it. And how my butt would not have been in danger if Max had not been a member of the CMI team."

While her teammates debated whether Max was a burden or blessing, her eyes drifted down the table to the neighbor family that the Carleighs had invited over to dinner so they could "meet the smart kids here to help us all."

The parents were frowning. It was clear they didn't like all the bickering.

Their baby daughter, on the other hand, looked like she thought the whole scene was hysterical. She was laughing and clapping and gurgling and knocking over her sippy cup.

She also had an incredible mop of curly hair, especially for a girl so young she wasn't even speaking words.

She reminded Max of Dorothy.

The girl in the photo Max had found tucked inside the suitcase. The suitcase that looked like it was part of a matching set that went along with the battered old luggage Max had carried through her entire life—until she lost it in the crazy car chase, escaping Professor Von Hinkle and his henchmen outside Oxford.

Max wanted to know more about Dorothy.

She wanted to go back to Princeton and the Tardis House.

She wanted to talk to Dr. McKenna.

So what was stopping her? The CMI wouldn't miss her. Max could hear them chattering about how much trouble she caused, almost as if she weren't sitting right there with them.

They'd be better off without her. They could do more good in the world without her. They'd be fine if she drove back to Princeton.

All she needed was a chauffeur.

# 50

Around two a.m., Max snuck out of her bed in the motel where the CMI had booked a block of rooms.

She slipped on her jeans, her rumpled Princeton sweatshirt, and her long trench coat.

"So long, Siobhan," she whispered to her snoring roommate. "You guys will do amazing things without me holding you back."

She tiptoed to the door and, as quietly as she could, twisted the knob. She stepped into the corridor.

An avalanche of ice cubes thundered in the distance.

Siobhan was still snoring. The tumbling ice from the machine across the hall hadn't woken her up.

Max went out a side exit. She couldn't risk traipsing through the lobby where the night clerk was on duty.

She hurried to the van.

Max knew that Leo would still be sitting in the front seat because Isabl said there wasn't "any room for him at the inn" when the team drove back to the cramped hotel from the farm.

Nobody spoke to Max on that ride. They didn't have to. She knew what they were thinking. Max Einstein was worse than a liability. She was a threat. With Von Hinkle and Ms. Kaplan out of the picture, the Corp would do what they'd always done: find somebody new to come after Max.

But she wouldn't be there when they came.

Max ran her hand up Leo's back and tapped the power button.

The synthetic bot whirred to life, clicking and clacking its plastic eyelids and pumping hydraulic fluid into its joints.

"Hello. Greetings. Welcome."

"Hey, Leo. It's me. Max."

"Yes. My facial recognition software indicated as much."

"Plot a course for Princeton, New Jersey. 244 Battle Road."

"Do you have authority to make this request?"

"Has anyone denied me access? Klaus? Hana? Ms. Kaplan? Oh, right. We can forget what she wants because she was a spy. Just plot the course, Leo."

"Very well, Max. It's good to be receiving commands from you again. It reminds me of our time together in London. I have plotted the course."

"Great," said Max, closing the driver's-side door. She ran around the front of the van, yanked open the door on the other side, and hopped into the passenger seat. "Let's roll."

"Where would you like to roll to?"

"244 Battle Road. It's why I asked you to plot a course."

"I see," said Leo. He giggled.

Max felt a tinge of guilt. Was she going to have to lie on top of playing a real-life version of Grand Theft Auto? It was a temporary theft, she told herself. Once she got to Princeton, she'd send Leo back. He could drive himself. He might even make it back to West Virginia before the group finished breakfast and headed over to the Carleigh place to implement some sustainable farming techniques.

"I'm leaving the CMI team, Leo." And then Max lied, for maybe the first time in her life. "Ben agreed that you would transport me to Princeton. It's my home. I think."

"Interesting," said Leo.

And then the electric hybrid van's engine shuddered awake.

"I will exit the hotel parking lot under electric power," said Leo. "It is silent. We don't want to wake the others."

*No*, thought Max. *We sure don't.*

And then she wondered: *Does Leo know that I'm, basically, stealing him and the van? Is his artificial intelligence that good?*

Probably.

After all, Klaus had been tinkering with it. And Klaus was a genius. All the kids on the CMI team were. Yes, they'd become Max's friends (her first real ones) but they'd do fine without her.

Better than fine.

Max kept telling herself that, hoping one day she'd actually believe it.

# 51

**Max slept for most of the four-hour ride.**

The usually chatty Leo remained silent. His sensors had probably picked up on the fact that Max was wiped out. She'd had a rough couple of days. Being demoted. Staring down a charging SUV. Helping Isabl line up a non-lethal takedown shot. Watching federal agents take Ms. Kaplan and Professor Von Hinkle into custody. Hearing how everybody would be better off without her.

About twenty miles outside of Princeton, Leo started monologuing. It woke Max up faster than a phone alarm set to sonar.

"The pull of home is strong," Leo said out of the blue. "Even for a non-sentient, theoretically unthinking creature such as myself. Your place of origin imprints in the deepest recesses of your memory chips, whether they be silicon like mine or brain cells like yours. Klaus tried to erase all of my Corp programming. And yet..."

"And yet what?" asked Max with a yawn. Leo sounded so human. He also sounded like he needed somebody to hear his story.

"Well, Max, I have deep memories. Core memories. Memories that cannot be erased. For instance, a certain refrain has wormed its way up into my prefrontal cortex and will not silence itself. 'Almost heaven, West Virginia. Blue Ridge Mountains, Shenandoah River.' West Virginia is *my* home, Max. The Corp built me there."

"Is there a robotics institute at West Virginia University?"

"Yes. But that is not my place of origin. I was built at the Corp headquarters. Deep in a West Virginia cave."

"You're sure about this?"

Leo nodded. "Yes. It has come back in bits and bytes, but I have reconstructed my origin narrative. West Virginia is my home. The Corp's, too."

"So that's why Ms. Kaplan wanted us to base our project outside Shepherdstown. So the Corp goons wouldn't have far to travel."

"Very considerate of her," said Leo.

"Yeah. Very."

Fifteen minutes later, the van, in electric engine mode, drifted down Battle Road. It was a little after six in the morning. The sun was starting to turn the eastern sky pink and blue.

"I'm going inside," Max said to Leo.

"Very well."

"You should drive back to the hotel in West Virginia. Hana and her team will need you today."

"I suppose you are correct. Good luck, Max. I hope you are able to reconstruct your own origin narrative."

"Thanks, Leo. It's been fun knowing you."

"I will take your word for that, Max, as Klaus has not yet programmed me to have fun."

The bot was giggling as Max climbed out of the van. There was a new sign posted in the front lawn announcing the "Battle Street Demolition Project." The building was scheduled to be knocked down in two days. The Tardis House would no longer keep time traveling into the future.

Max remembered the combination for the electronic pad securing the back door.

She creaked it open and stepped inside the empty house. It was even dustier than she recalled. When she closed the door, all the light disappeared. The sun might be rising but the windows were still boarded over. She turned on the

234

tiny West Virginia Mountaineers souvenir LED flashlight she'd picked up at the hotel's small gift shop the day before. She swung its bluish beam around the room. The tattered suitcase was still leaning against the wall.

And so was Albert Einstein.

# 52

**Max rubbed her eyes in disbelief.**

When she did, she dropped her miniature flashlight.

It didn't matter. She could still see Dr. Einstein. It was almost as if he were glowing with an aura shimmering around him. He was dressed as Max always pictured him. Baggy khaki pants. Frumpy sweater. He was casually packing tobacco into the bowl of a pipe.

"If I could travel back in time," he said, holding up his unlit pipe, "this would be the one thing I would attempt to change. Filthy habit, Max. Avoid it at all costs."

Max couldn't tell if she was imagining this, the way she imagined the Albert Einstein in her head, or if she was actually talking with the real Albert Einstein who had, somehow, transported himself from the past into the future, which just happened to be Max's present.

"Of course," said Einstein, "going back in time is practically impossible. Yes, general relativity provides some scenarios for doing so, but they are difficult to achieve. You would have to travel at the speed of light in a vacuum."

"Not possible. At least not yet."

"True. However, my equations show that an object moving that fast would have both infinite mass and a length of zero."

"I, uh, wouldn't want to do that," said Max.

"Now, wormholes *are* possible between points in the space-time fabric. But these minuscule tunnels would only be suitable for the passage of very tiny particles. Not you or I, Max. And the passageways would collapse very quickly. If they actually exist. No scientist has actually observed one . . . not yet anyway. Maybe you will, Max. Maybe that will be your future."

"So I can't go back to 1921 and meet my parents?"

"I'm afraid not. Not until you find the way. Currently, there is no practical or physically possible way for you to return to this space at that time. And I'm certain that many people around the world are very glad for that fact."

"Excuse me?"

"Well, Max, if you were able to travel back in time, you might warn your parents about their time machine."

"They wouldn't listen to me. I was just a baby. I couldn't even speak."

"Ah, but if you went back, you would go back as the you that you are today even though you would be visiting parents who only knew you as a small child. That version of you would also exist in that piece of the space-time fabric."

Max grimaced. "Me showing up would probably freak everybody out."

Einstein nodded. "Plus, if you shut down the time machine and never came into the future, you would never do all the great things you've already done in your life. We wouldn't be standing here right now if you went back in time and convinced your parents to dismantle their project. This version of you would no longer exist because your time leap would never have happened."

Max stared at Einstein.

He brought his hands up to his head and mimed fingers exploding out of his curly white hair in slow motion. "Mind blown, yes?"

"Yes."

"Your mother and father were brilliant, Max—both of them with their sights focused on the future because they knew that's where you, their only daughter, would live."

"So they built a time machine and it actually worked? It sent me forward?"

"And a little to the left," joked Einstein. "I suppose that's how you ended up in the basement of the house next door. Seems there is space dilation as well as time dilation. The space in one wrinkle of time will not line up precisely with the same space in another wrinkle of time. It's all relative."

Einstein tucked his pipe into the pocket of his sweater.

"I have to go, Max. Your parents have purchased a lovely orange cake and fresh strawberries. It's my favorite dessert. I mustn't keep them waiting in the kitchen any longer."

"Wait," stammered Max. "If I can't go back to the past, how can you? How can you go back to a 1921 kitchen for strawberries and cake?"

Einstein grinned and waved good-bye.

His image vanished like a fade-out at the end of a movie.

*This was all in my head,* Max told herself. *That was a long drive from West Virginia. You're still half-asleep. You're still dreaming.*

The door behind her creaked open.

Sunlight streamed into the room.

"Hello, Dorothy," said a soft voice behind her.

It was Dr. Shannon McKenna.

# 53

**"Did you see him?" Max asked excitedly.**

"See who?" said Dr. McKenna.

"Albert Einstein! He was right here. Standing against that wall. Near the suitcase."

She didn't seem fazed by Max's wild statements. "Ah, yes. The suitcase."

"Was I hallucinating? Maybe I was having a dream while I was wide awake?"

Dr. McKenna grinned. "Those are the best kind of dreams, aren't they? The wide-awake ones. That's what imagination is, Max. Allowing yourself to dream with your eyes open. To create things that aren't really there. But, remember this, nothing in this world—not that window, or door, or even these floorboards—came into existence until somebody imagined that it could."

"Imagination is more important than knowledge," mumbled Max, reciting her favorite Einstein quote.

"Indeed."

"So, why did you call me Dorothy?" Max asked. "When you came into the room, you said, 'Hello, Dorothy.' Why?"

"Because, Max," said Dr. McKenna, "I believe that's who you really are. I believe you are the daughter of the young professors Susan and Timothy. The little girl they, very accidentally, transported into the future during their 1921 experiments, which, of course, were done while Albert Einstein was visiting the Princeton campus."

She walked over to the suitcase.

"I have been researching what went on in this house for decades, Max. In your visits to this place, have you discovered any other furniture? Any other objects from the past?"

Max shook her head. "No. Just the suitcase. And the photo that was tucked inside. I took the photo."

Dr. McKenna nodded. "As I imagined you might if you ever returned to what, in 1921, was your home. Why do you think we left one single piece of luggage locked up in an abandoned building? It was a sentinel. A guard keeping watch. Sitting there, waiting for the appearance of a Dorothy at some point in the future. Because the only one who would seek out this antique piece of luggage would be the one who left this house in 1921 with a matching piece."

"So you knew when I came here that first time?"

"Yes." She gestured toward a miniature security camera in a smoky dome hidden in a corner of the plaster molding where the walls met the ceiling. "I'm just glad you showed up before the bulldozers. The town and university have grown tired of my insistence that this house could help us prove that time travel is possible."

"Can you tell me more about my parents?" Max could hardly contain herself. Finally, she would get answers to the questions she had her whole life.

"They were true geniuses. Engineers who could take the theoretical and make it practical. I was going to write my doctoral dissertation about them and what they had been rumored to have achieved. But my committee steered me away from the subject. Until you showed up, I lacked proof that they had done anything except generate a good deal of gossip." She reached into her coat. "I do have a photograph of them. And you, Dorothy."

She showed Max a fading portrait of an intense couple from the 1920s proudly posing with their infant daughter.

"I'll make you a copy," said Dr. McKenna.

The photo. Mom, Dad, Baby Dorothy.

. I think I just discovered how
you can time-travel into the past:
look at an antique photograph.
    Are these really my parents?
            Is that really me?

"Thanks."

*BANG BANG BANG!*

Suddenly, something was knocking three times against the plywood covering a side window. Hard! The sound startled Max and the professor.

"What in the blazes?" said Dr. McKenna.

"It could be the Corp," said Max.

"What?"

The rapping repeated. Three solid knocks, a pause, then three more.

"Other people are looking for me, too," Max told the professor. "Bad people. Stay here."

"No way. I'm going with you."

Max shook her head. "I don't want the Corp hurting anyone else because of me. And they will. Stay."

Dr. McKenna nodded. "Be careful."

Max found her flashlight and crept out of the living room, through the kitchen and into what, long ago, might've been a dining room.

"Max?" came a tense voice from outside the window. "Can you kindly open the window?"

It was Leo.

"I thought I told you to drive back to West Virginia!" Max whispered harshly.

"I can't do that, Max."

"I'm sorry, Leo. I need to stay here. In Princeton."

"You can't," whispered the bot on the other side of the plywood. "Princeton is not safe."

"Yes, it is."

"No, Max, it is not. Not for you and not for me."

"And why not?"

"Because Dr. Zacchaeus Zimm is next door."

# 54

**Dr. Zimm stood on the front lawn of 246 Battle Road.**

Two muscular gentlemen in black suits that strained against their bulletproof vests stood behind him. All three wore sunglasses to fight off the beams of morning sunshine piercing through the leafy canopy of trees.

"I lived here once," Dr. Zimm announced. "Princeton is an excellent place to do advanced research. It's really quite easy. All you have to do is steal it from the professors doing all the grunt work."

The two beefy men behind him—Edward and Wilhelm—chuckled.

"This house was our headquarters. We made the Corp a fortune, something they have never forgotten. It's also where I first met little Max Einstein. She was a baby crawling around the floor, circling an antique suitcase." He shook his head remembering that remarkable morning twelve years in the past.

"And you suspect Miss Einstein has returned to the scene of your first meeting?"

"I don't suspect it, Edward. I know it. You see, Professor Von Hinkle assumed the Corp had shipped me off to a re-education facility in northern Greenland when, in fact, they sent me home to Boston so I might keep tabs on Von Hinkle. His taking over the pursuit of Max Einstein was his orientation and evaluation period with the Corp. His trial run."

"How'd that work out for him?" joked Edward, who already knew the answer to his question.

"Not very well, Edward. Professor Von Hinkle is currently awaiting trial in a rather dismal West Virginia jail cell. The Corp's lawyers will most likely arrange for his release and then his disappearance. Professor Von Hinkle cost us dearly. His blunders exposed the deepest asset we had at the CMI. Ms. Tari Kaplan's cover, which took many years to build, was blown in one foolish afternoon."

"So, they gonna ship Von Hinkle up to Greenland?" asked the other guard with a satisfied grunt.

"Most likely, Wilhelm. But first, I hope to conduct his exit interview. Truth serum will be involved. The kind that makes one drool uncontrollably." Dr. Zimm grimaced.

"So, how'd you know Max Einstein came poking around this house?" asked Edward.

"We secretly installed tracking beacons in Professor Von Hinkle's squadron of attack drones. The drones flew to this location before Miss Einstein cleverly eliminated them from the equation."

"She's a smart kid," said Wilhelm.

"She's a genius," said Dr. Zimm, stroking his gloved hands over his bald dome. "Fortunately, I'm even smarter. Her unrelenting quest for knowledge about her past—who she is, where she came from—will, undoubtedly, bring her back to this house once again. You see, I ran an extensive psychological profile on—"

"Excuse me?" A man in a bathrobe came out to the front porch. He eyed the three men in black suits and dark sunglasses standing on his neatly trimmed lawn. "Can I help you gentlemen?"

"I certainly hope so," said Dr. Zimm, with what he thought was a pleasant smile. He sometimes forgot how pointy his teeth were. "We're looking for my daughter. She's about twelve. Curly red hair? Floppy trench coat?"

The man didn't answer.

"Her name is Max."

Still nothing from the man in the bathrobe.

248

"Tell me, sir," said Dr. Zimm, quite cordially, "do you have children?"

The man nodded. "Two. Boy and a girl."

"Are they, by any chance, tweens or teenagers?"

"Maybe." The man had a very skeptical look on his face. He inched his right hand into the robe's deep hip pocket. Zimm assumed he was a professor. An egghead. Therefore, he would not be reaching for a weapon. Most likely his phone so he could call 911.

"Well, then," said Dr. Zimm, doing his best to sound amiable, "you know how dramatic they can act at that age. My daughter is twelve. She ran away from home a few days back. We think she may have come to Princeton to visit this house."

"Why?"

"Because we used to live here. When she was a baby. Twelve years ago."

"Twelve years ago?" said the man.

"That's right." Dr. Zimm attempted another smile.

"That's when the corporate espionage ring was operating out of this house," said the man, angrily. "You people stole one of my ideas."

"I assure you, sir, neither I nor my daughter—"

The man wasn't listening. He was calling the police.

"Gentlemen?" Dr. Zimm said to his two associates. "We should depart."

"You want we should eliminate the snitch in the bathrobe first?" asked Wilhelm.

Dr. Zimm sighed. "Yes. I suppose we should."

"Help!" The man frantically shouted into his phone.

But it was too late.

# 55

**Max hurried back to the living room.**

"Dr. McKenna? I have to leave. Now."

"Who was that at the window? Someone from this Corp you mentioned?"

Max shook her head. "No. I mean he used to work for the Corp. Now he's with us. The CMI."

Dr. McKenna looked confused but Max really didn't have time to explain how Leo was a humanoid who used to be called Lenard. She didn't have time for anything.

"There is a very evil man next door. His name is Dr. Zimm."

Dr. McKenna nodded. "The name is familiar from my research. He was part of the spy cell that operated out of 246 Battle Road a dozen years ago. Very despicable individual."

"Well," said Max, "he hasn't gotten any better with age. He's here looking for me."

"Then why is he next door?"

"Space-time dilation."

"Excuse me?"

"When my parents zapped me into the future with their time machine, which I imagine was set up down in the basement?"

"That's right," said Dr. McKenna. "How'd you know?"

"I saw the scorched floor. Anyhow, when they flipped the switch to put me on fast forward, I ended up in the basement of the house next door because of some wrinkle in the fabric of space-time."

"So, this Dr. Zimm could further confirm my time travel hypothesis. He was a witness to your time jump!"

"True," said Max. "He might help you out. Or, he might haul you off to a remote re-education facility first. Some place super chilly. Word of advice from *my* research? Stay away from him, Dr. McKenna. I gotta run."

"But he's looking for you."

"Next door. Not here."

"But how will you and your friend outside escape?"

"Good question. I was hoping you could maybe help us with some kind of diversion."

"I could call the police."

Now someone was knocking on the boarded-up *front* windows.

"Max?" Leo whispered through a crack where the plywood met the siding. "Dr. Zimm is otherwise engaged at the home next door. An ugly altercation with the owner of the property. We have a narrow window of opportunity! I predict a sixty-five percent probability of a safe and incident-free extraction if we initiate said extraction immediately."

"Your friend sounds a little...odd," said Dr. McKenna.

"Yeah," said Max. "He's a robot."

"A what?"

"Thanks for the pictures. I gotta go."

"Will you be coming back? I'd like to meet this robot. I'd like to interview you some more."

Max shook her head. "No, thanks. I think I've spent enough time dwelling on my past. It's time to start working on the future. Nice meeting you."

Max threw open the creaky window and put her shoulder to the plywood. Nails squealed.

"Sorry about this," she said to Dr. McKenna, right before she gave the sheet of warped wood a good swift kick. Now there was an opening wide enough for Max to crawl through.

Leo was standing in the field of weeds that used to be the home's flower beds. He had his arms extended.

"Jump!" he said. "I will catch you."

"Um, thanks. But no thanks."

Max toppled out of the window and crashed to the ground. She also made a lot of noise doing it.

"Hurry!" said Leo, probably too loudly.

Because, next door, up on the front porch, Dr. Zimm and two giants in black business suits stopped trying to kick open the front door of 246 Battle Road.

They were more interested in all the commotion in front of 244.

"Hello, Lenard," called Dr. Zimm. He smiled creepily. "Hello, Max. I'm so glad we could all have this lovely reunion."

He turned to his two goons.

"Seize them!"

# 56

Leo popped open a panel in his torso.

A half dozen sizzling bottle rockets came streaking out of his chest.

Dr. Zimm and his two henchmen dropped to the ground as the fireworks exploded overhead.

"I now extrapolate that we have a twenty-two second jump on our pursuers," said Leo, running for the van parked at the curb.

Max ran after him.

"Who gave you a weapons system?" she shouted.

"Klaus," said Leo, yanking open the driver's-side door of the van. "But it is not a weapons system. It was intended as a surprise for the Fourth of July."

"Drive!" yelled Max after she jumped into her seat

255

and slammed the door shut. In the distance, she could hear sirens approaching. Somebody *had* called the police. Maybe Dr. McKenna. Maybe whoever lived in the house next door. Maybe they didn't like the Corp hit men trying to kick down their door at dawn.

"Destination?" asked Leo as they raced up the street.

Max checked the rearview mirror. Dr. Zimm and his two associates were scrambling to their feet and climbing into their vehicle—a sleek black sedan with black tinted windows.

"West Virginia," said Max. "Eventually. For now, initiate Isabl Driving Protocol."

"Are you certain about that, Max?"

"Yes. Punch it!"

The hard drive inside Leo's plastic head made grinding noises. He was accessing the defensive driving database that Klaus had loaded into his backup system just in case Leo ever needed to drive like Isabl (which was, basically, like a maniac speed demon).

"The Corp vehicle is three hundred yards behind us," Leo reported as they whipped through a series of switchbacks and screeched into a tire-burning turn. "Local police have been summoned to 246 Battle Road and are now in pursuit of the Corp vehicle. Should I initiate more evasive actions?"

"No. We need to help the cops. Slow Dr. Zimm down so they can pull a PIT maneuver."

"Sorry," said Leo. "I have not been provided with information about PIT maneuvers. I could tell you about Pitt University. Or peach pits…"

"PIT stands for pursuit intervention technique," said Max, climbing over her seat and into the back of the van. "They'll use basic physics to stop Dr. Zimm's car. They'll tap his rear wheels at an acute angle with their front wheels. That'll cause the Corp vehicle to skid sideways. We're going to use basic chemistry to help them out."

"Fascinating," said Leo.

"Did you and Isabl grab that diesel fuel when we stopped at the rest area?"

"Yes. Charl suggested we might need it for field generators. The five-gallon canister is stored in the area behind the rear bench."

"Perfect," said Max. "That means it's close to the tailpipe, too!"

Max climbed over the rows of seats and made it to the back of the van. She could see the Corp sedan gaining on them. She could also see swirling roofbars in the distance. The police were in pursuit.

Max screwed the nozzle onto the diesel fuel can. She popped open the rear vented window and shoved the nozzle through the gap in the corner closest to the van's exhaust pipe. Leo's rapid acceleration and maniac moves had caused every part of the car's internal combustion system to heat up quickly—including the tailpipe.

"Reduce your speed, Leo!"

"Reducing speed, Max."

The van slowed.

Max tilted the gas can and started pouring diesel fuel. It sloshed and splashed all over the place, including on the hot tailpipe. In a flash, a cloud of white smoke billowed up behind the van, creating a thick smokescreen that forced Dr. Zimm's car to slow down.

The police knocked the Corp sedan into a spinout. It twirled like a top until it came to a stop.

Max and Leo flew out of Princeton and headed for the highway, driving one mile per hour underneath the maximum posted speed limit for every stretch of road they traveled.

Because they didn't want any other police vehicles using a PIT on *them*.

# 57

"Thank goodness you did that, officers!" said Dr. Zimm as he and Wilhelm climbed out of the back seat of the car.

Edward was stuck behind the steering wheel, an inflated airbag pinning him in place.

"He was driving like a maniac!" Dr. Zimm continued. "Worst Uber ever."

"Thank you for rescuing us, officers," added Wilhelm, even though he was so huge, he didn't look like he'd ever need rescuing from anything.

"You two don't know the man behind the wheel?" asked one of the police officers.

"No, sir," said Dr. Zimm. "But I do know that his

four-star rating on this ride-sharing app is a complete exaggeration."

"If you don't know him," the officer said to Wilhelm, "how come you two are dressed exactly alike, with the black suit, white shirt, and skinny black tie?"

"Coincidence?" said Dr. Zimm, answering for Wilhelm. "Now, if you will excuse us."

A black SUV crunched slowly up the road.

Dr. Zimm gestured toward it. "We're late for an urgent appointment. We've already summoned a new car. It's a Lyft this time, thank goodness. Not an Uber. Thank you again, officers."

They hurried into the new Corp vehicle as quickly as they could. The police seemed to be buying the idea that Edward, trapped behind the wheel of his getaway vehicle, was just a rogue Uber driver.

"Drive!" Dr. Zimm barked the instant he and Wilhelm landed in the back seat. "Be quick about it! But don't do anything rash to draw the police officers' attention."

The man behind the wheel obeyed. Dr. Zimm waved politely as the SUV cruised past the dented sedan where the officers were deflating the airbag, helping the dazed Edward out of the driver's seat.

"You kind of threw Edward under the bus back there, Doc," said Wilhelm as they pulled away.

"So?" said Dr. Zimm. "Lose one asset to save two. It's standard Corp procedure. Do you have some problem with that, Wilhelm?"

"Nope," said Wilhelm. "Just wish I'd thought of that whole Uber thing. That was smart, Dr. Zimm. Very smart."

"Sir?" said the new driver, touching his earpiece.

"Yes?" said Dr. Zimm.

"Phone call coming in from HQ. They say it's important."

"Put it on speaker."

"Yes, sir." The driver jabbed a screen on his dashboard console.

Dr. Zimm leaned forward. "This is Dr. Zacchaeus Zimm. How may I be of assistance?"

"This is command and control at the Cave," said a clipped and efficient female voice.

The Cave was what those who worked for the Corp called their secret mountain hideaway.

"Go on," said Dr. Zimm.

"Please proceed to the Sarnoff Princeton Heliport. A chopper is waiting to ferry you and your team back here."

"But Max Einstein is within my reach. She is only five minutes ahead of us. Given what I know about her psychological profile, I'm certain she is heading back to West Virginia to rejoin her CMI team. The girl has guilt issues and what I call delusions of goodness. Her protectors, Charl and Isabl, aren't currently with her. Only Lenard, the automaton. With your assistance, tracking satellite feeds covering all major roadways leading back to—"

"There is no need for that, Dr. Zimm," said the woman from Corp headquarters. "We have acquired a new CMI asset. We don't need to chase down Max Einstein on the open road. This new asset will deliver her to us."

"Is that so?" said Dr. Zimm, rubbing a thoughtful hand across his bald head. "And how, exactly, did we acquire this asset?"

"The old-fashioned way," said the woman with just the hint of a smirk in her voice. "They called us."

# 58

Max and Leo were both surprised when no sleek sedans or hulking SUVs shadowed them on the long drive back to West Virginia.

"Any drones overhead, Leo?" Max asked.

"None that my rudimentary radar has picked up."

"Huh," said Max. "Maybe Dr. Zimm decided to call it quits."

Leo rotated his head sideways to give her a look. (As a robotic driver, he really didn't need to keep his eyes on the road because his processors were linked to the vehicle's external sensors and satellite navigation system.)

"Dr. Zimm does not give up," Leo said calmly. And then, of course, he giggled.

"What do you mean?" asked Max.

"It is not in his nature to surrender. Notice how, even when replaced by Professor Von Hinkle, he remained, as you say, in the game?"

"True. So, why'd he just let us leave Princeton? Why isn't the Corp using its access to spy satellites and surveillance drones to track us down? Come on—we're driving down an interstate highway..."

"My internal navigation system informs me it is the speediest route, even though there are tolls involved."

"That's not my point. Why did Dr. Zimm just let us go if he never gives up?"

"Because," said Leo, "I extrapolate, with ninety percent certitude, that he expects that we are doing what we are, indeed, doing. Returning to the motel outside Shepherdstown. Dr. Zimm *wants* us back in West Virginia."

"Your old home," Max muttered.

"Precisely. Because it is also home to the Corp."

Max was torn. Part of her wanted to pull the CMI team out of West Virginia, immediately. Part of her wanted to finish the hunger project. After all, what good was calling yourselves the Change Makers Institute if you were too terrified of the big bad Corp to make any changes in the world?

"Leo, can you communicate with Charl and Isabl?"

"Yes, via Klaus. I have him on what he called 'speed dial.'"

"All right. Tell Klaus to alert Charl and Isabl to beef up security for the team. The Corp, clearly, knows where we are and what we're doing. We should be better prepared for another attack like the one at the Carleigh farm."

"Oh, I agree," said Leo. "I might suggest that Charl and Isabl bring on more troops as the Corp has many assets in the area."

"And we don't," said Max, her mind fast-forwarding the way it did when she played chess. She needed to plot out all her possible moves and all her opponent's potential counter-moves. The best chess masters can see fifteen moves ahead, maybe twenty.

Max could calculate twenty-five.

"Tell Klaus that he and I need to chat over text. Set up a good time."

Max, who had just spent way too much time obsessing over her own past, wanted Klaus to do a little tinkering with Leo's memory board. To delve back into the robot's past a little. To give him back some of the old "evil Lenard, Corp lackey" edge he had when he was playing for the other team. Klaus may need to consult with Charl, too.

"Very well," replied Leo. "I have texted Klaus. Might I inquire as to what the topic of your private discussion will be?"

"Sure. Because we're going to talk about you, Leo."

"I would be flattered—if that emotion were available to me."

"Well, you should be. I have a feeling you're going to help us shake off the Corp once and for all."

"It would be my great honor, Max." The robo-boy sounded noble. Almost heroic.

But then he did that giggle thing again and totally blew the mood.

# 59

"We got your message," Charl told Max as they marched up the corridor with Isabl and Leo. "We've set Klaus up with everything he might need."

"Great," said Max. "Thanks."

Both Charl and Isabl had compact semiautomatic weapons draped over their shoulders.

"Hana says we're pulling out," said Isabl.

"I guess that's one option," said Max.

Max and Leo had made it, without incident, back to the motel where the CMI team was staying. Now they strode into one of the motel's small conference rooms where everybody was gathered around a long wooden table.

"The Carleigh family wants nothing more to do with us," said Hana, sounding slightly ticked off at Max. She

268

was seated in a padded office chair at the head of the table. "After what happened with the Corp coming after you and Isabl's sniper shot and the police... it's all too much."

"I'm sorry, Hana," said Max. "I didn't mean to sabotage your first project as team leader."

"Well, you did anyway, didn't you?"

"Hey," said Max, tired of feeling guilty and defensive, "I wish Dr. Zimm and the Corp weren't constantly trying to track me down but, guess what? They are. Yeah. You heard that right. Dr. Zacchaeus Zimm's back in the hunt. Leo and I bumped into him back in Princeton."

"Well," said Klaus, "I for one am glad you're back safely."

"Thank you," said Max.

"I meant Leo, not you," said Klaus. "Kidding. I'm glad you're both here. Come on, Leo. I want to take a peek under your hood. Make sure you're operating at one hundred percent of your full potential before we box you up and ship you back to who knows where."

Klaus shot Max a wink that no one else saw. On the drive through Maryland on the way to West Virginia, Max and Klaus (using Leo as an intermediary) had their private conversation, texting back and forth, plotting improvements for the "new-old" Leo/Lenard. They looped Charl and Isabl into the text conversation, too.

Max looked at her friends seated around the table. "Just

269

because the Corp wants to stop us doesn't mean we have to stop doing good work in the world."

"Are you nuts?" said Keeto, directing his fury at Max. "You might as well paint a target on your back. And while you're at it, paint one on all our backs, too."

"Whoa," said Siobhan. "Take a chill pill, boyo."

"Seriously, Keeto," added Tisa.

"I am serious," said Keeto. "As long as Max Einstein is on this team, our lives are in constant jeopardy."

"Maybe so," said Max. "But you know whose life was also in constant jeopardy? Albert Einstein's. The Germans were after him. The anti-communists in America, too. But you know what he said? 'There is no greater satisfaction for a just and well-meaning person than the knowledge that he has devoted his best energies to the service of a good cause.'"

"Well put," said Siobhan.

"I agree," said Tisa.

Annika was the only one not saying much. She kept clacking keys on her laptop computer, scowling at the screen. Toma, seated beside her, had a sheet of data spread out in front of him.

"Well," said Keeto. "I'm not Albert Einstein. And neither are you, Max."

"Enough," said Hana. "We're leaving. As team leader,

I've decided: This mission is officially canceled. Annika? Toma? How goes the planning?"

"We're arranging air transportation for everybody," said Toma. "It's a logistical nightmare, getting everyone back to their home countries..."

"But," said Annika, "we've put together a plan efficiently coordinating all the many moving parts: ground transportation and flight times for all CMI personnel as well as details about shipping gear, equipment, and, course, Leo back to Jerusalem where—"

"That's it!" said Max.

"What's what?" sneered Keeto.

"The answer to world hunger!"

# 60

Max started pacing up and down along the side of the conference room where there was a whiteboard mounted to the wall.

She grabbed a marker.

"Okay," she said. "Hear me out. Try to see what I'm seeing."

The other kids were staring at her. Charl and Isabl were smiling. They'd seen Max get lost in one of her thunderclouds of discovery before.

"On the drive back, we passed the Carleigh farm. Crops were rotting in the field. They won't be good for anything but compost this time tomorrow."

"We advised him to take his produce to the local farmers' market," said Hana.

"Which is when?" countered Max. "Saturday?"

Hana nodded.

"Too late." Max made a big X on the whiteboard. "It'll all be rotten by then. This is what's been nagging at me." Max tapped her temple. "The big, simple idea. It keeps bubbling up, trying to present itself."

"What?" asked Tisa, eagerly. "What is it?"

"Hunger is not a food issue," said Max, writing the words boldly across the board. "It's a logistics issue. There's enough food in the world. It's just not where it's needed. This hunger crisis involves the whole global supply chain. Storage, transportation, packaging, shipping, roads, tracking—everything." She moved to where Annika and Toma were working on the travel planning. "You guys—when you saw we had a travel problem, you broke it down into manageable steps. That's what logistics is all about. The detailed coordination of a complex operation, involving lots of people, facilities, and supplies. Instead of restaurants and grocery stores and rest area snack shops throwing away perfectly good food, we need software and infrastructure to help us move it to where it is needed most!"

"Brilliant," said Siobhan.

"May I say something?" asked Charl.

"Of course you can," cracked Keeto. "You're carrying a loaded weapon, aren't you?"

Many hands make light work!

It's like apple-picking with a purpose.

"Work is the only thing that gives substance to life."
—Albert Einstein

"What Max is talking about reminds me of a project we have in Israel called Leket."

Charl sounded nervous. He wasn't used to speaking in public.

"Not only does Leket rescue healthy surplus foods from parties such as weddings and bar mitzvahs, but they also rescue the crops from the fields before they rot. A number of farms have signed up for the program and there are regular events, calling on the public to come out, to rescue the remaining vegetables and fruits, and transfer the food to where it is needed most."

"We could do that on a small scale here in West Virginia," said Max. "If we can prove that it will work here, then others can take the idea and expand on it all over America. All over the world! We need to use data and become decision scientists!"

Heads started nodding around the table.

"So, um, we're not going home?" said Keeto.

"No," said Hana. "Max's idea has merit. I like that concept: Decision Scientist. What do we need to get started?"

And the group started brainstorming.

"Trucks!"

"A warehouse!"

"Refrigeration."

Max let the team take over. She jotted down all their ideas on the board.

She also couldn't help but smile. It felt great to be looking forward toward a brighter future instead of focusing so much on her own murky past.

# 61

**The next day, things were even better.**

The Corp and Dr. Zimm had made no move to snatch and grab Max. Charl and Isabl, with the help of the local police, had established a tight security perimeter around the motel. Hana, who was still the official team leader, had a real "there's no I in team" attitude.

Keeto was the only one still grousing about "being stuck in the boondocks."

"On our next assignment, can we please do something in a city? Some place with, I don't know, a Starbucks or something?"

The rest of the group was working on their phones and computers. Identifying farms and restaurants with surplus food. Looking for "distribution points," like the loose network of food pantries operating out of churches.

"We can link them all together," suggested Siobhan. "Deliver our produce the way supermarkets deliver produce to their chain of stores."

"I'm also talking to bakeries and restaurants," said Tisa.

"We're going to need a solid transportation partner," said Hana, who'd been looking into the local trucking companies.

"UPS would be great," said Toma. "Check this out." He called up some research he'd discovered online. "By obsessively tracking its drivers, UPS found 'a significant cause of idling time resulted from drivers making left turns, essentially going against the flow of traffic.' So now, UPS drivers are encouraged to make nothing but right turns. That one little change has saved one hundred million gallons of gas and reduced carbon emissions by one hundred thousand metric tons since 2004!"

"They'd be awesome partners," said Max.

"But remember the point you made yesterday, Max," said Hana. "We need to start small. UPS isn't going to jump on board until we take this notion to the national or international level."

"That's not our job," said Annika. "It would be impossible for the CMI to manage an operation of that scope."

"You're right," said Max. "We're the proof of concept. Other groups are better equipped to scale it up."

"So," said Hana, "I found a very promising trucking company. Hambrecht Hauling. They're locals and keen on contributing to the community."

"They sound perfect!" said Max. "Let's sign them up."

"They want a meeting first," said Hana. "I told them how Leo can pilot vehicles, turning them into autonomous automobiles or, for this company, self-driving trucks."

Max grinned. "So, they want to see Leo in action before they start working with us? They want a peek at tomorrow's technology today?"

Hana nodded. "Precisely."

"Sounds like a small price to pay for such a big win," said Keeto. "Take the meeting, Hana."

"They want to meet Max, too."

"Really?" said Max. "Why?"

"Maybe because Mr. Carleigh told everybody in a three-county radius about what went down at his farm," suggested Klaus, swaggering into the conference room with Leo. "Face it, Max. You're famous."

Charl and Isabl came into the room, too. They looked intense.

"We just picked up some Corp chatter," said Isabl.

"As did I," said Leo.

Charl took over the briefing. "The Corp is planning an orchestrated attack at eleven hundred hours. They're sending their hit team here to grab Max and Leo."

"It's ten o'clock now," said Hana, glancing up at a clock on the wall.

"Might be a good time for Max and Leo to not be here," suggested Keeto.

"We could go talk to your truckers," said Max. "Take Leo. Charl and Isabl can lock down this location. If the Corp goons show up you can politely tell them, sorry, Max and Leo aren't here."

"And you wouldn't be lying," said Klaus. He nodded at Charl and Isabl. They nodded back.

"Do it, Max," said Charl.

"No problem," said Max.

She turned to Klaus.

"Thanks for checking out Leo." She shook his hand. "We need him firing on all cylinders today. He has to impress the owners of a local trucking company with his mad driving skills."

"But I don't drive," said Leo. "I simply pilot the craft."

"Well, pilot us to this address," said Hana, putting a slip of paper in front of Leo's eyes so he could scan it into his memory.

And while she did that, Max pinned onto the lapel of

her trench coat the little robot button Klaus had slipped her during their handshake.

Then she checked to make sure she had everything she might need stuffed into the coat's deep pockets. Because she had a feeling that the most important chess game of her life had already begun.

# 62

Leo was behind the wheel of the van, turning it, once again, into an autonomous, self-driving automobile.

Hana and Max shared the first bench of seats in the back.

"Once we organize the trucks, the hunger problem will be solved," said Hana. "We can move on to our next project."

"I don't think it will be 'solved,'" said Max. "At least not on a global basis. But, with the right algorithms and software to track, monitor, and keep the food flowing, it'll be a good start. A logistics model that others can duplicate."

"Whatever," said Hana, rather dismissively. "I'm just eager to move on to my next big thing."

Max nodded and smiled.

Because Hana had revealed herself when she said "my next thing" instead of "our next thing."

All that "no-I-in-team" stuff she'd been spouting? Another part of her act. And, Max had to admit, it was a pretty good act.

But not good enough to fool Max.

"You know," Max said aloud, "I'm kind of glad it's you and not Keeto."

"Excuse me?" said Hana.

"I mean, he whines and complains a lot, but he's brilliant. He's designing most of the software for the food redistribution idea. So, Hana—what did they offer you?"

"Who?"

"The Corp."

"Shall I terminate this journey?" asked Leo from the front seat. "Do you anticipate trouble, Max?"

"Why are you asking her?" snapped Hana. "I'm the Chosen One."

"Wow," said Max with a small laugh. "Is that what this is about? You like the title? The prestige?"

"I am going to turn this vehicle around," said Leo.

"No," said Max. "Don't. We'd probably all die if you

did. What do they have tracking us, Hana? An armed drone?"

Hana's nose twitched. "They weren't specific. But, yes, they do have access to armed drones with extremely lethal capabilities."

"That means they'd blow you up, too, Hana," said Max. "Nice people you're working for."

"Be quiet! Pull in here, Leo. Now!"

"Max?" said Leo.

Max shrugged. "Do what Hana says, Leo. After all, she's the Chosen One. The one who *chose* to betray the CMI."

Leo drove the van through the gates of a rusty, chain-link fence topped with barbed concertina wire. He piloted the vehicle across the pothole-pocked parking lot of what looked to be an abandoned warehouse. A freshly painted sign (much newer than anything else on the premises) declared this to be Hambrecht Hauling.

"Nice touch," said Max sarcastically. "Very realistic sign. Oh, and that bogus communications intercept about the Corp coming to get Leo and me at precisely eleven hundred hours? That was a slick move, too. You completely eliminated Charl and Isabl from the equation."

Now Hana was grinning. "Well, Max, as you might have forgotten, I am brilliant, too."

Max saw a burly man armed with a small submachine gun step onto the loading dock.

Hana powered down her window. "Are you Wilhelm?"

The man nodded.

He came down a short flight of concrete steps and yanked open the passenger-side door.

"You really did think of everything!" said Max. "You kept the front seat open for your friend Wilhelm with the semiautomatic rifle and put me in the seat diagonally behind him."

"So I can shoot you if you misbehave," said Wilhelm, aiming his weapon at Max's heart. "Drive!"

"To the Cave?" said Leo.

Wilhelm seemed surprised by Leo's response. "You remember the way?"

"Oh, yes, Wilhelm. Thanks to a recent reboot and refreshment of my core data, I remember many things from my past. If you like, you can call me Lenard."

"Whatever you say, tin can."

Leo, as always, kept cool. "Calculating route to the Cave. Anticipate arrival in forty-four minutes."

"So drive," snarled Wilhelm.

"Yes, sir, Wilhelm. Right away, Wilhelm."

Wilhelm smiled. "Robots. You gotta love 'em. They'll do whatever you tell 'em to do."

He chuckled.

Leo giggled.

And the van drove off toward the rolling green mountains on the horizon.

# 63

"Dr. Zimm will be happy to see the two of you, that's for sure," said Wilhelm.

"Hana and me?" said Max, playing dumb (which was easy for her to do because she was so smart).

"No. You and Lenard here. The Corp shelled out a ton of money to build this bot. They'll be glad to have him back on the job, doing what he was designed to do. And you, Maxine? Dr. Zimm says you and your brain are gonna bring in billions!"

"I'm sure he will offer you a very attractive compensation package," said Hana. "As they have for me."

They still had a way to go until they reached the Cave. And Max needed Leo to drive as slowly as possible, without either Hana or Wilhelm recognizing what he was doing. So she kept up the conversation with Hana.

"What will you be doing for the Corp, Hana?" she asked innocently.

"Creating the true cure for worldwide hunger," said the eager young botanist. "GMOs. Genetically modified organisms. Plant-based biotech. It's what I was working on when the CMI first came knocking at my door. With genetic engineering, I can create plants that are twenty, even thirty percent larger than current breeds. That means more food can come from every acre of farmland. We'll do more to alleviate starvation in the third world than you and your ridiculous logistics idea."

"And you'll probably make a lot of money, too," said Max.

"So? Money isn't a bad thing. Look at Ben. Who says our 'benefactor' is the only teenager who can be a multibillionaire? This is what Ms. Kaplan and I would discuss late into the evening some nights after the rest of you had already gone to bed. She helped orchestrate my takeover of the CMI. Of course, you helped, too, Max. We knew we could play on your disdain of exams and testing. Ms. Kaplan has your psychological profile. She knew how to play you like your hero, Dr. Einstein, played his violin."

"Then," said Max, "I guess that means she knew how to play you, too, Hana."

The ride was quiet and frosty after that exchange.

"Projected arrival at the Cave in fifteen minutes," Leo chirped after ten minutes of stony silence.

"Can't you drive any faster?" said Wilhelm.

"Of course I can. However, this stretch of road is heavily policed. It is what they call a speed trap. If we were to be pulled over and an officer happened to notice what I take to be an Israeli-made Uzi nine-millimeter semiautomatic carbine in your lap, there might be questions."

"Just drive," said Wilhelm. "And shut up."

Exactly fifteen minutes later, the van passed through a security gate and came to a stop in a clearing where the access road dead-ended at the sheer bluff of a mountain.

Suddenly, the side of the mountain slid sideways, exposing a brilliantly lit subterranean highway.

"Where are all the security guards?" asked Leo.

"The humans?" said Wilhelm. "They've been replaced. By *those* guys."

A sleek white robot that looked like the top of a rocket on wheels whizzed past the van.

"Dr. Zimm is waiting for you in the boardroom sector," said Wilhelm. "You remember where that is?"

"Of course," answered Leo. "I remember everything."

"So," said Max, as the van crept deeper into the cavern, "this is where you'll be working?"

"You, too," said Hana. "Although I suspect I'll have an office while you'll have a cell. They'll probably park Leo in a garage."

The van traveled another six hundred yards and pulled to a stop underneath an elevated, circular glass room. All seven chairs around the ornately carved wooden table were filled.

"You might recognize some of those faces upstairs, Max," said Leo. "That is the Corp's board of directors. They are all multibillionaires and captains of industry. Leaders of big pharma, big media, big…"

"Keep your big mouth shut," snapped Wilhelm. "They prefer to remain anonymous."

Max grinned. She could see why.

Respectable business leaders forming a secret consortium and, basically, ruling the world while simultaneously destroying it? That wouldn't make for good public relations. Exposing them—putting their faces on TV or the internet—might be the best way to shut the Corp down. It's like somebody once said: sunlight is the best disinfectant.

"Everybody out," barked Wilhelm.

"Gladly," said Hana.

"I suppose we must do what we are told to do," said Leo.

"Exactly," said Max.

They both climbed out.

And Dr. Zimm giggled when he saw them.

# 64

So that's where Leo gets it, thought Max when she was face-to-face once again with the evil man whose teeth were too big for his skull-like face.

"Hello, Max," he said with manic glee. "So good to see you again. You, too, Lenard. Welcome home."

"It's almost heaven," remarked Leo. "West Virginia. Blue Ridge Mountains. Shenandoah—"

"Yes, yes," said Dr. Zimm. "That was the first thing the techies taught you, I'm told. Wait here. Max and I are needed upstairs."

"Where is my office?" asked Hana.

"Oh, it's not here, dear. We wanted to put you someplace special. Wilhelm?"

"Sir?"

"Kindly organize an appropriate relocation package for our friend Hana. Perhaps our facility in the Sahara Desert. She is of no further use to us."

"Wait! What about—"

Wilhelm dragged Hana away.

"I despise GMO food," Dr. Zimm said with a snicker to Max. "Corn cobs the size of watermelons? Revolting. Lenard, you will wait here. And don't even think about escaping. You see those security bots whirring up and down the tunnels? They are highly weaponized and equipped with facial recognition software. They have both of your faces loaded into their memories."

Leo stood stock still at the base of the steps leading up to the boardroom. "I will wait here as requested, Dr. Zimm. I do not want to incur the wrath of my robotic cousins."

Fortunately, none of those patrolling cousins were close to the staircase leading up to the boardroom.

"Excellent. Follow me, Max. The board is eager to finally meet you. I think you will enjoy hearing what they have to propose."

Max clanked up the circular steps behind Dr. Zimm, stuffing her hands into the pockets of her trench coat. Not because she was pouting, but because she was doing one last gear check. She also checked out the ductwork snaking its way into the sealed-off, soundproof plastic room where the

Corp's board of directors waited patiently for Dr. Zimm to deliver his prized catch.

Dr. Zimm tapped a rapid series of numbers onto a security keypad. A glass wall whooshed sideways to become a sliding door. Max followed the man who had discovered her crawling around in the basement of a house on Battle Road in Princeton when she was just a baby. They stepped into the command and control center of perhaps the most nefarious organization currently doing business anywhere on Earth.

The door swooshed shut behind them.

"So. This is the famous Max Einstein," said a woman seated on the far side of the circular table. Max immediately knew who she was. Her face was constantly featured in all the top business magazines and cable TV channels.

"I won't beat around the bush. We have a proposition for you, little lady," said a bloated man with a thick Texas accent. Another famous face. He owned TV networks. Sports teams. An energy drink company. "A business proposition. Because that's what we are. Businessmen."

"Except Mrs. Winthorp, or course," said Max, letting the woman on the far side of the table know that Max knew exactly who she was. "And Ms. Henriques there."

"I stand corrected," said the man with the twang, trying his best to sound friendly. "We're all business *people*. So, here's the proposition, Maxine. You help us develop our quantum computer and bring it to market, fast. We'll give you thirty percent of the gross profits. Which you won't think is gross at all!" He chuckled at his terrible joke.

"And of course," said Dr. Zimm, "as your agent, I will take fifteen percent of your thirty percent."

Max nodded.

"Seems fair."

"Sure as shootin' it's fair," said the Texan. "We'll give you all the resources you need. A lab, technicians, you name it."

"And," added Dr. Zimm, "if you do a good job, I'll tell you everything I know about where you came from."

Max tapped the robot pin on her lapel.

"You mean how you found me crawling around in the basement of the house you and a bunch of corporate spies were renting on Battle Road in Princeton? Lenard has already told me everything you know, Dr. Zimm."

The glass wall swooshed open.

"It's true," said Leo, bursting into the room. His chest compartment was open and bristling with high-tech weaponry. "And, yes, as you might have noticed by the number of firearms currently pointed at you, I've had serious upgrades since I left your employ. I also have excellent telescopic vision and was able to memorize the security code you tapped on the pad, Dr. Zimm. That young man Klaus is a genius. Not as brilliant as Max, here, but a true genius. Now then, all of you. Up against the far wall. Move it. Unless, of course, you are interested in dying."

And then, like always, he giggled.

# 65

All the board members cowered at the far side of the circular room.

Max was amazed at the number of pointy weapons—rifles, rocket launchers, maybe even a flamethrower—jutting out of Leo's chest. Charl, the weapons expert, had gone a little overboard helping Klaus turn the robot boy into a war machine.

"Target coordinates are locked in," said Leo with some of his old Lenard menace.

"You know you won't get far!" said Dr. Zimm, his hands raised over his head. "The security bots will destroy you. If just one of them sees your face—"

"They'll think it's Halloween," said Max.

She reached into the deep right pocket of her floppy

trench coat and pulled out two rubber masks. One was Frankenstein. The other was the current president of the United States. She tossed the Frankenstein mask to Leo. "You be Frankenstein. I always wanted to be president."

"Your wish is my command, Max."

They took turns squeaking on their rubbery masks.

"We're going to lock you folks in," Max told the group of billionaires, her voice muffled by the mask. "But we're not cruel. Release Hana and, five minutes later, we'll release you. Deal?"

No one answered. They just glowered and glared at the girl who thought she could outfox some of the foxiest business executives in the world.

"Okay," said Max. "Think about it. Like I said, release Hana and we'll open this door."

"Your Wi-Fi is quite good down here," remarked Leo. "Especially for being inside a mountain. I commend you on your technical expertise. The lock and I have already established a wireless connection that cannot, I'm sad to say, be overridden. Klaus did that for me, too. As I said, the boy is brilliant."

"Let's go, Leo."

"This isn't over, Max!" shouted Dr. Zimm as she and Leo backed up toward the open glass door.

"You're right. It's not over. Not yet. But soon."

Max exited first. Leo kept his arsenal of weapons trained on the leaders of the Corp. Finally, he stepped out of the circular room. The man from Texas lurched toward the door but it slid shut with a glassy *thunk* before he could reach it.

With their rubber masks thwarting all the facial recognition software in the security bots, Max and Leo breezed down the steps and headed for the exit.

"Leo?" said Max, looking up at all the pipes and conduits worming their way across the cavern's craggy ceiling. "Which one of those ducts feeds fresh air into the boardroom?"

"Accessing blueprints," said Leo. Klaus had restored everything he'd previously erased about Lenard's past with the Corp. "The middle one."

"Great. I need you to hoist me up. You see that vent? I'm going to put something inside it. Something that's been stewing in a jar for a long time."

"If I might inquire, what exactly is it?"

"A little encouragement for Dr. Zimm and the others to free Hana so we'll open the door to that airtight, soundproof boardroom."

Max removed the jar that she'd been carrying in her

pocket since that night she visited the drugstore in Princeton. She'd been putting together the moves for this end game since before she even knew that's what she was doing.

"It's a stink bomb," she explained. "Match heads contain hydrogen sulfide. Soaked in ammonia. Mix them together, let them sit for a few days, and you have ammonium sulfide. The vapor I'm releasing into the air duct is the same as hydrogen sulfide gas, what you might call rotten egg smell. It's also flammable. So let's hope none of those bigwigs fires up a cigar."

"Not to worry," said Leo. "The Cave is a completely smoke-free environment."

"Well, it's not going to be a stink-free environment much longer. Give me a boost."

Hydraulics whirring, Leo hoisted Max up toward the ceiling. She popped open the vent in the duct, set her jar inside, and twisted off the cap.

"Bring me down!" she said, trying her best not to breathe through her nose.

"Does it smell bad?"

"Horrible!"

"Then I am glad the Corp never gave me olfactory sensibilities."

They dashed up the tunnel, running past several of the robotic security guards. None of them recognized their faces. And they had no orders to fire on Frankenstein or the president of the United States.

Max and Leo finally made it to the sealed cave entrance where Wilhelm was waiting for them.

He had Hana.

He also had his submachine gun.

# 66

"Open the door, Wilhelm," said Max, pulling off her mask.

"Ha! Forget it, kid," Wilhelm snarled. He jabbed the muzzle of his weapon into Hana's ribs.

Hana was sobbing. "I'm so sorry, you guys," she blubbered.

"As you should be," said Leo, who'd also taken off his mask. "Wilhelm, have you forgotten that your hostage betrayed us? Why should we want to protect, save, or rescue *her*?"

Wilhelm paused to think about that. He even lowered his weapon slightly.

But it was enough.

It gave Leo a clean shot.

The door in his chest flew open and out sprang the twin barbed probes of a laser-guided Taser stun gun. Wilhelm's limbs spasmed as the electric pulse convulsed him. He dropped his weapon, which clattered on the stony floor. He toppled to his knees. Quivering from the electric jolt, he flopped sideways and scooted around the dusty floor in kicking circles.

"What's the door code?" screamed Hana. "We need to get out of here."

In the distance, alarm sirens started whoop-whooping.

"Evacuate the facility," purred a way-too-calm pre-recorded voice. "Evacuate the facility."

"Release Hana!" came the voice of Dr. Zimm over the loudspeakers. He coughed some. Gagged, too. "Open this door, Max! Open this door immediately!"

"Guess the stink bomb must've done its thing," said Max.

"What is that stench?" asked Hana, sniffing the air. "Rotten eggs?"

"Hydrogen sulfide gas," said Max, trying not to breathe through her nose. The smell had worked its way into the air filling the tunnel, too.

She scooped up some dust from the floor and blew it across the keypad controlling the sliding stone wall entrance. "You see it, Leo?"

"Indeed I do. And, might I say, that is a very clever trick."

"Thanks. We'd better hurry. Wilhelm isn't going to stay incapacitated for much longer."

"Indeed. Allow me to do the honors."

Leo scanned the dusted keypad, deciphered the code by following the fingerprint pattern, and punched in the correct sequence of numbers. The solid rock wall slowly slid open.

"Now open the boardroom door," Max told the bot.

"Boardroom door is now open," reported Leo.

Hana ran out into the sunshine as soon as the gap between the moving door and the stone wall was large enough.

"Hello, Hana," said Charl, waiting on the other side.

"I'm sorry. I didn't mean to—"

"Yes, you did," said Isabl. "Keeto? Take her to our vehicle. Lock her in."

Keeto led Hana away.

Max stepped out of the mouth of the Cave and smiled because the craggy courtyard between the entrance to the

Corp's cavernous headquarters and their guardhouse was filled with people. The whole CMI team, of course. Mr. Carleigh and a bunch of his farmer friends. Folks from the network of church food banks. Several police officers (who had the guardhouse attendant in the caged back seat of one of their cruisers). And, most important, TV crews from CNN, Fox News, MSNBC—every news outlet there was.

"How'd Leo do?" asked Klaus.

"Fantastic!"

Klaus clapped Leo on the back. "Atta boy!"

"And the remote control was a brilliant touch," said Max, tapping her robot lapel pin. "Came in handy."

"He was an excellent tracking device, too," said Charl. "Well done, Klaus."

Klaus shrugged. "What can I say? I'm a genius. Then again, we're all geniuses! Everybody on the team. Well, except Hana. She's smart but dumb, know what I mean?"

Max laughed. "Yes, I do." She turned to the waiting press corps. "Cameras up, guys. The stars of our show should be coming out any minute."

Hacking, coughing, covering their noses with fancy handkerchiefs, the seven bleary-eyed members of the

Corp's board came stumbling out of the cave, gasping for fresh air.

Dr. Zimm was the first one out.

And the first one captured on the footage that aired on every news channel that night.

## 67

**The next week was a busy one.**

The media had a field day exposing the corporate titans operating a "shady, greed-fueled organization known as the Corp." Reporters exposed how many "horror stories around the globe" were connected to the group and its leaders. Many lost their day jobs with some of the world's largest, best-known companies.

Some of the ex-Corp members threatened Max and the CMI: "This is phony news. Fake allegations. Those ignorant children will pay dearly for what they're trying to do to us and our reputations!"

"You think any of them will go to jail?" wondered Keeto, watching the corporate big shots and their lawyers on TV.

"Doubtful," said the somewhat cynical Siobhan. "The big dogs never have to pay for their crimes."

Dr. Zimm was taken into federal custody for attempted kidnapping. The FBI also wanted to talk to him about some twelve-year-old corporate espionage charges from his time in Princeton.

Ben bought Hana a one-way ticket home to Japan. He made sure the airline knew she would prefer the vegan meal option.

The CMI team might have to look for a new member. Maybe a biochemist who wasn't so focused on growing genetically altered soybeans the size of grapefruits.

In the meantime, Max stayed focused on the smooth operation and logistics flow of the food collection and distribution system they'd set up in their small corner of West Virginia.

It turned out that UPS was eager to partner with the CMI after all. Algorithms were written. Computer programs were running. Food that used to go to the landfill was now being saved. And, most important, that good food was getting to where it was needed most.

It was a model that could be replicated—all over the world!

"Thanks, Max," said Sam, the hungry young girl Max had met on her first trip to the church food pantry. Her

" The destiny of civilized humanity depends more than ever on the moral forces it is capable of generating."
—Albert Einstein

family was able to go home with shopping bags filled with nutritious food that they'd picked off grocery store–style shelves.

Sam was also able to grab a Honey Bun.

Because what's dinner without dessert?

With the operation running so smoothly (Annika, the logic whiz, played a huge role), Max was able to accept an invitation from Ben.

He wanted to do another lunch.

In Princeton.

# 68

Ben had been able to use his influence (and his money) to delay the demolition of the Tardis House.

So that's where he and Max had a catered meal around a simple table covered with crisp linen.

"I, uh, made a significant contribution to the university. They own this building," Ben explained. "The bulldozers will, you know, wait. And, with a little more financial encouragement, Professor Shannon McKenna might be able to continue her research into the mind-blowing work that was done here back in 1921."

Max smiled. "By the couple who might've been my parents?"

"Exactly! That is so cool, Max. You're a time traveler. The first one I've ever met. Do you remember anything from 1921?"

"Nope," said Max. "I'm not even sure it's true."

"It might be," said Ben. "You know what Sherlock Holmes says. 'Once you eliminate the impossible, whatever remains, no matter how improbable, must be the truth!'"

"Okay," said Max, putting down her cucumber sandwich. "Let's do a little thought experiment, Ben. What if I really am Dorothy, the only child of the professors who lived here a hundred years ago? Everybody says they were geniuses. Einstein thought they were even smarter than him because they could take his theories and give them a practical application. Maybe Susan and Timothy were my mom and dad, and I inherited my smarts from them. What if I climbed into a suitcase while their time machine was whirring away down in the basement? What if I came here from 1921? What if I almost met Albert Einstein when I was a baby?"

"Let's find out!" said Ben. "We could work out what really happened back then. Wouldn't it be exciting to get those answers?"

Max shook her head. "No. It would be interesting, but I know one thing that's certain: We can't travel backward in time. We can't live in the past, either. We can only look forward. To the future. And Ben? That's where things get really exciting!"

# MAX EINSTEIN IS AT IT AGAIN!

She's trying to solve the world's problems and escape the evil claws of the Corp at the same time. Max continues to recruit help from her hero, Dr. Albert Einstein, and her friends at the Change Makers Institute (CMI) to solve one of the planet's worst problems: world hunger. Unfortunately, Max's focus is torn in multiple directions—solving the problem of world hunger, escaping the Corp, and finally discovering who she really is.

Although Max's adventure may be over, you can re-live moments from the book with these activities and create your own reading adventures. Let's get going!

# CHANGE MAKERS INSTITUTE BUSINESS CARDS

The Change Makers Institute (CMI) continues to help others by finding ways to improve their quality of life. CMI business cards can spread the word about the team and how they help others!

Become the CMI's marketing manager and create a business card for someone on the CMI team. Be sure to include:

- ✎ their name
- ✎ a picture (drawn by you)
- ✎ hometown
- ✎ accomplishments
- ✎ a quote that will sum up their purpose in life

## Example:

12-YEAR-OLD GENIUS
HOMETOWN: PRINCETON, NJ

### Max Einstein
MEMBER OF THE
CHANGE MAKERS INSTITUTE (CMI)

"Only a life lived for others is a life worthwhile."
–Albert Einstein

ACCOMPLISHMENTS:
- solar panels for electricity in Africa
- filtration system for clean water in India
- working on solving world hunger

Don't stop there! Create your own business card. What skills and accomplishments do *you* have? Find a quote that shares more about you and your passions. You can include a fake phone number and address. Do you have a fake website and email address? Include those as well! And remember…creativity rocks!

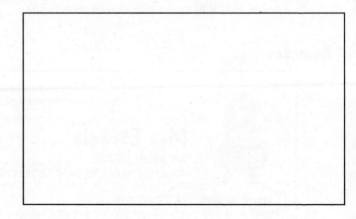

# FRIENDSHIP FACTOIDS

Max finally finds friends on the CMI team. They are there for her when she needs them the most. For example, they surround her when Professor Von Hinkle attempts to steal her. They travel to many different places to help Max assist those in need. How well do you know Max's friends? Could you determine which friend is described here just by reading facts about them? Read the clues to solve the friend mystery. Write their name in the box. Then, using the letters above the number, complete Albert Einstein's quote about friendship.

## CLUES

1. I am an expert in robotics and pride myself on my vast knowledge of technology. I believe "go big or stay home," especially when we are solving the world's problems. I love food! One time, I accidentally helped the Corp when I accepted a gift, which was a phone. However, I will make sure not to make that mistake again!

— — — — —

2. I do not need a last name. I am skilled in martial arts and have an accent that is from somewhere in Eastern Europe. I possess many skills, including lassoing evil-doers from the Corp. Some on the CMI team may call me a "quiet addition."

— — — — —
2

3. As a computer scientist from California, I am destined to be "the next Steve Jobs." There is no code I cannot crack. Others may see me as short-tempered, but it is just because I have no patience for wasting time.

— — — — —
4

4. I am a friend of Max's, and it's very unlikely I would ever betray her. My family is considered wealthy and resides in Africa, where I became a biochemist. I hate taking any tests and always try to have a sunny smile on my face.

— — — —
1

5. I am a master of formal logic and believe "without logic, none of those other sciences could function." I am from Germany and enjoyed eating my feast at the World Hunger Banquet. I am very good at coordinating plans, like trips to return home.

— — — — — —

"However rare ___ ___ ___ ___ love may be,
           1    2    3    4

it is less so than ___ ___ ___ ___ friendship."
            1    2    3    4

—Albert Einstein

**Answers:** 1. Klaus, 2. Charl, 3. Keeto, 4. Tisa, 5. Annika
Quote: "However rare rare **true** love may be, it is less so than **true** friendship."

# THUNDERCLOUDS OF DISCOVERY

Max loves to work through ideas and find solutions to the world's problems. As the ideas flow through her, she brainstorms what she knows. She investigates theories originally tested out by Albert Einstein and all the possible ways the problem can be solved. Charl and Isabl refer to this brainstorming as "Max's thunderclouds of discovery." Look at the list of issues that face our world today. What "thunderclouds of discovery" can you come up with? Write or draw on the clouds how *you* could possibly solve the problem. Remember, you are "blue-sky thinking" (p.148), which means there is no limit to your ideas. Think BIG! Be creative! The sky's the limit!

## LOCAL ISSUES

★ Lonely elderly neighbors
★ Crowded animal shelters
★ Homelessness
★ Neglected town gardens
★ Overbuilding of houses and apartments

# GLOBAL ISSUES

★ Climate Change
★ World Hunger
★ Poverty
★ Inequalities
★ Ocean Conservation

Issue _____

What is Known?

How can I help?

Issue _____

What is Known?

How can I help?

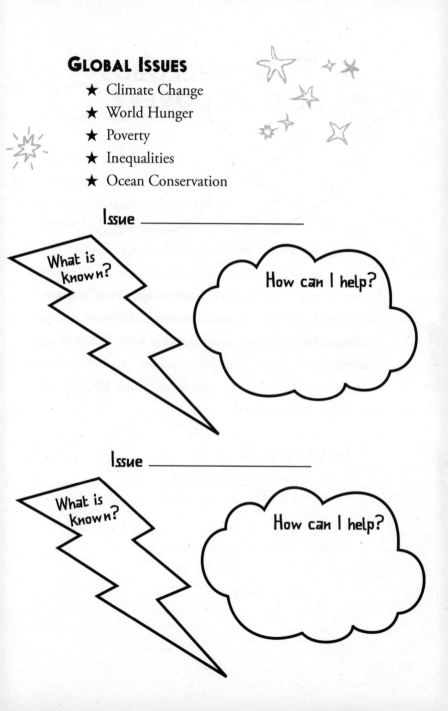

Issue _____

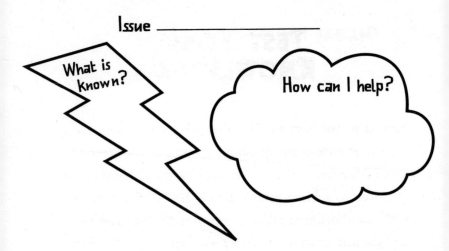

What is known?

How can I help?

Now that you are inspired with ideas, you can help out in your community! Like Albert Einstein said, "Keep on sowing your seed, for you never know which will grow—perhaps it all will."

# TEST YOUR KNOWLEDGE

Now that you have finished the book, are you up for a challenge? How many questions can you answer correctly about *Max Einstein Saves the Future*? Answer 8 out of 10 questions to achieve genius status, just like Max and the CMI team! Before sneaking a peek at the answer key, try to find the correct answer in your book. As Max said, "Education is training the mind to think." Don't let the questions trick you...your book is there to help train your mind and find the answers.

1. **During the world hunger banquet, Ms. Kaplan shares statistics about world hunger. What percent of the world lives in a middle-class country?**
    a. 10%
    b. 20%
    c. 70%
    d. 35%

2. Where is the Royal Albert Hall?
   a. West Virginia
   b. New Mexico
   c. London
   d. Oxford

3. Who became the new leader when Max was demoted?
   a. Annika
   b. Hana
   c. Toma
   d. Klaus

4. Which Avenger bad guy was Professor Hinkle compared to?
   a. Ultron
   b. Loki
   c. Thanos
   d. Dr. Doom

5. What was the show Darryl referenced when talking about the house on Battle Road?
   a. *Sherlock*
   b. *The Crown*
   c. *The Bodyguard*
   d. *Dr. Who*

6. Finish the quote, "Imagination is more important than _____ ."
    a. knowledge
    b. playing
    c. learning
    d. education

7. What name did Dr. McKenna call Max?
    a. Dolly
    b. Susie
    c. Annie
    d. Dorothy

8. Where is the Corp's hideaway?
    a. West Virginia
    b. New Jersey
    c. Oxford
    d. Texas

9. What was Hana going to do when working for the Corp?
    a. Create genetically modified organisms
    b. Open a plant-based supermarket
    c. Build robots that spy on people
    d. Plant trees all over the world

**10. What problem was the CMI team working on in _Max Einstein Saves the Future_?**

    **a.** Climate change

    **b.** Irrigation systems

    **c.** World hunger

    **d.** Solar panels

# ABOUT THE AUTHORS

**James Patterson** is the internationally bestselling author of the highly praised Middle School books, *Not So Normal Norbert, Unbelievably Boring Bart, Katt vs. Dogg,* and the I Funny, Jacky Ha-Ha, Treasure Hunters, Dog Diaries and Max Einstein series. James Patterson's books have sold more than 385 million copies worldwide, making him one of the biggest-selling authors of all time. He lives in Florida.

**Chris Grabenstein** is a *New York Times* bestselling author who has collaborated with James Patterson on the I Funny, Jacky Ha-Ha, Treasure Hunters, House of Robots, and Max Einstein series, as well as *Word of Mouse, Katt vs. Dogg, Pottymouth and Stoopid, Laugh Out Loud* and *Daniel X: Armageddon.* He lives in New York City.

**Beverly Johnson** is an LA-based illustrator and character designer. She loves sketching, cats, and chocolate.

# Read the Middle School series

Visit the **Middle School world** on the Penguin website
to find out more! **www.penguin.co.uk**

GET YOUR PAWS ON THE

HILARIOUS DOG DIARIES SERIES!

# ALSO BY JAMES PATTERSON

## MIDDLE SCHOOL SERIES

The Worst Years of My Life (*with Chris Tebbetts*)
Get Me Out of Here! (*with Chris Tebbetts*)
My Brother Is a Big, Fat Liar (*with Lisa Papademetriou*)
How I Survived Bullies, Broccoli, and Snake Hill
(*with Chris Tebbetts*)
Ultimate Showdown (*with Julia Bergen*)
Save Rafe! (*with Chris Tebbetts*)
Just My Rotten Luck (*with Chris Tebbetts*)
Dog's Best Friend (*with Chris Tebbetts*)
Escape to Australia (*with Martin Chatterton*)
From Hero to Zero (*with Chris Tebbetts*)
Born to Rock (*with Chris Tebbetts*)
Master of Disaster (*with Chris Tebbetts*)

## I FUNNY SERIES

I Funny (*with Chris Grabenstein*)
I Even Funnier (*with Chris Grabenstein*)
I Totally Funniest (*with Chris Grabenstein*)
I Funny TV (*with Chris Grabenstein*)

School of Laughs (*with Chris Grabenstein*)
The Nerdiest, Wimpiest, Dorkiest I Funny Ever
(*with Chris Grabenstein*)

## DOG DIARIES SERIES
Dog Diaries (*with Steven Butler*)
Happy Howlidays! (*with Steven Butler*)
Mission Impawsible (*with Steven Butler*)
Curse of the Mystery Mutt (*with Steven Butler*)
Camping Chaos! (*with Steven Butler*)

## HOUSE OF ROBOTS SERIES
House of Robots (*with Chris Grabenstein*)
Robots Go Wild! (*with Chris Grabenstein*)
Robot Revolution (*with Chris Grabenstein*)

## JACKY HA-HA SERIES
Jacky Ha-Ha (*with Chris Grabenstein*)
My Life is a Joke (*with Chris Grabenstein*)

## OTHER ILLUSTRATED NOVELS
Kenny Wright: Superhero (*with Chris Tebbetts*)
Homeroom Diaries (*with Lisa Papademetriou*)

Word of Mouse (*with Chris Grabenstein*)
Pottymouth and Stoopid (*with Chris Grabenstein*)
Laugh Out Loud (*with Chris Grabenstein*)
Not So Normal Norbert (*with Joey Green*)
Unbelievably Boring Bart (*with Duane Swierczynski*)
Katt vs. Dogg (*with Chris Grabenstein*)

For more information about James Patterson's novels,
visit www.penguin.co.uk